CHASING THE DRAGON

Unlocking the Stars' Secrets

ECHO SABLE

TABLE OF CONTENTS

Chapter 1: A Dying Astrologer 1

Chapter 2: The Dying Astrologer's Final Words 17

Chapter 3: Flora's Interpretation...26

Chapter 4: Harlan's Strange Experience 33

Chapter 5: Black Gilded Box 49

Chapter 6: Response from the Observatory...........................88

Chapter 7: The Answer to the Evil Sign 106

Chapter 8: A New Theory of Life..123

Chapter 9: Secrets in Empty Boxes 146

Chapter 10: Harlan's Weird Behavior 164

Chapter 11: Harlan's Major Discoveries 183

Chapter 12: Journey to Another Land...................................209

Chapter 13: Fate 224

CHAPTER 1

A DYING ASTROLOGER

That night, the heavens unleashed a torrential symphony upon the city, as if the very fabric of the sky were unraveling. For over half an hour, the deluge persisted, drenching the streets with a relentless cadence.

At the opera house entrance, a crowd huddled under its grand awning, rendered impotent by the downpour cascading from the eaves in a thousand tiny waterfalls. The cacophony of the rain was a relentless roar, with each passing car sending geysers of water into the air, adding to the chaos.

As the final notes of the opera faded, the heavy rain had already begun its encore, trapping the elegantly attired patrons within the theater's confines. Their sartorial splendor — crisp tuxedos and flowing gowns — seemed almost absurd against nature's wrath. Reluctant to brave the elements, they gathered at the entrance, swelling in numbers until they spilled into the lobby.

On nights like these, the air was thick with heat and humidity, a palpable force pressing down on the throng. Yet the rain showed no mercy, intensifying with each passing minute, a curtain of water showing no sign of lifting.

Opera was not to my taste—its languid pace clashed with my sensibilities. The protagonists, seemingly on death's door, would pause inexplicably to sing their plight for an eternity. Yet, Flora adored it. Her delight was evident, her face still aglow with the performance's afterglow, unfazed by the inconvenience of the storm. She remained lost in the echoes of the stage.

After a mere ten minutes of waiting, impatience gnawed at me. I loosened my tie, the constriction mirroring my growing frustration. "The car's not far," I proposed. "We'll get a bit wet, but why linger here?"

Flora's silence spoke volumes, her tacit disapproval palpable. Yet, my resolve hardened. The theater dimmed its lights, casting us in shadow. Outside, the streetlights lent an ethereal glow to the rain, the droplets sparkling like jewels. A sudden nostalgia gripped me, a yearning for the reckless abandon of youth when the rain was an adventure, not an inconvenience.

Ignoring Flora's reluctance, I seized her hand and began to weave through the crowd, murmuring polite requests for passage. As we neared the exit, my path was blocked by a man, a pillar of obstinacy.

"Why push? It's still raining hard outside，" he barked, his voice booming over the rain's din. He was a formidable presence, a middle-aged man of stature and status, his impatience mirroring my own.

I met his glare with a calm defiance. "Please, make way. I choose the rain."

His lips twitched, but he relented, allowing us passage. I led Flora past him, muttering my disdain. "Some people fear the rain like it's a curse. He'd probably skip his father's deathbed to stay dry."

Flora shot me a reproachful glance, her eyes chiding. As if on cue, the man let out a disgruntled growl.

Then, cutting through the murmur of discontent, a voice called out, clear and unmistakable: "Ash Morris!"
The unexpected shout pierced the ambient noise, turning heads. I paused, curious to unmask the source of this bold interruption.

Through the crowd, a figure emerged, barreling toward me with little regard for decorum. His presence was unmistakable—Harlan Brown, a friend whose penchant for the uncanny was unmatched. Our past exploits, particularly the "charcoal" incident, had cemented his reputation as a seeker of the extraordinary, a man whose imagination knew no bounds.

Harlan Brown, with a boldness that belied his slight frame, squeezed past the middle-aged man. His hand reached out, shoving the man with unexpected force. I stifled a laugh, fully expecting the man to retaliate. Yet, to my amazement, the man stumbled back a step and merely gaped at me, eyes wide with shock, as if witnessing an apparition.

Curiosity piqued, I wondered why the man chose silence over confrontation. But before I could ponder further, Harlan Brown reached me, his voice booming over the noise: "Ash, finally! I've been searching for you. There's something urgent I need to discuss."

His voice cut through the air, drawing the attention of those around us. "Alright," I replied, eager to deflect the spotlight, "let's talk while we walk."

Harlan Brown hesitated, incredulous. "Walk? In this downpour?"

I had little patience for his theatrics. "Find shelter then. I'm leaving," I declared, turning on my heel and striding into the rain.

Behind me, Harlan Brown's voice rose again, desperate now. "Ash, you'll regret ignoring this. It's something bizarre, something you need to hear!"

I knew well enough the nature of Harlan Brown's so-called bizarre tales — wild imaginings spun from the mundane. He once spent a month scrutinizing a scrap of paper blown into his path, convinced it was an extraterrestrial communiqué.

Flora and I descended the stone steps into the storm, the rain pelting us mercilessly. Within moments, we were drenched, but the exhilaration of it all was a welcome distraction. I grabbed Flora's hand, splashing deliberately through the puddles, laughter bubbling up as water sprayed around us.

Flora leaned in, her voice a whisper amid the deluge, "Someone's following us."

I didn't need to look back. "Let Harlan Brown get soaked," I chuckled, unfazed. We continued our watery escapade, the rain a curtain between us and whatever mysteries Harlan Brown thought he held.

"It's not Harlan Brown," she said, her words stopping me in my tracks. We stood beneath a flickering street lamp, the rain cascading over us like a veil. Flora's soaked silhouette was ethereal, her hair plastered to her skin, droplets tracing paths down her cheeks. In that moment, she seemed like a vision from a dream, and I couldn't resist leaning in to kiss her. She blushed, her lips curling into a shy pout. But then, she subtly nodded her head, hinting for me to look behind.

I turned to see a figure standing behind us, drenched and disheveled. Not Harlan Brown, but the same middle-aged man from before. Rainwater streamed down his face, blurring his features, and he blinked furiously, trying to focus through the deluge. Recognition dawned on me, and I burst into laughter, the absurdity of the situation not lost on me. I tilted my head back, welcoming the rain as it mingled with my laughter.

Flora nudged me gently, her voice a soft admonition. "This gentleman seems to have something to say."

The man wiped his face, hesitating as if searching for the right words. My laughter subsided, and I raised my voice above the storm. "What is it you want to say? I appreciate the reminder about the rain just now."

His discomfort was palpable, and Flora, ever the diplomat, suggested, "Our car is just ahead. Perhaps we can talk there."

Before the man could respond, an imposing black RV pulled up beside us. A driver, uniformed and visibly flustered, leaped out, stammering, "Master, you··· you···"

The driver's shock was almost comical, his words stuttering into silence, overwhelmed by the sight of his soaked superior.

The man, now identified as the "Master," finally found his voice. "Mr. Morris?" he asked, his tone urgent even amidst the downpour.

I nodded, the rain splashing off my brow, adding to the surreal atmosphere.

"Could you please come with me? There's someone who desperately wishes to see you. He's⋯ dying." His voice cracked, and I felt a tug at my conscience. "I'm not used to asking for favors," he admitted, his pride clearly chafed by the request.

The weight of his words sank in. A dying man's final wish—what kind of person would I be to refuse? Yet, his reluctant humility rubbed me the wrong way. "Then perhaps you should start getting used to it," I replied, my words sharper than intended.

I turned to leave, but Flora's gentle touch on my sleeve halted me. Her eyes held a silent plea, urging empathy where my stubbornness reigned. I turned to face him, and the sight was striking—his face was drenched, the rain mingling with his features in a way that made it seem as though he were weeping, each drop a tear cascading down his cheeks. The raw vulnerability in his eyes was undeniable.

With a sigh, I nodded to Flora, acknowledging her silent request.

The middle-aged man sighed with a weary resolve. "Mr. Morris, please, get in the car first." His voice carried a note of urgency, and he moved to open the door, holding it open with a kind of reverential insistence.

The uniformed driver seemed trapped in a loop of disbelief, his voice rising once more in a futile echo, "Master, you, Master, you!" It seemed to be the only phrase he could muster in his state of shock.

Flora offered a polite "thank you" and stepped into the car, her poise unruffled by the rain. I followed her into the vehicle, and the middle-aged man climbed in after us, taking a seat opposite us in the spacious RV. The interior was lined with white seat covers, an antiquated touch that suggested the owner's conservative tastes. As we settled in, the covers absorbed the rainwater from our clothes, leaving damp imprints behind.

The driver quickly took his place behind the wheel, his voice still tinged with disbelief, " Master..."

"Home," the middle-aged man instructed, his tone brooking no argument. The engine purred to life, and we eased forward, the headlights cutting through the relentless downpour.

Seated across from me, the middle-aged man was finally revealed in the dim light. Nearing sixty, the rain had etched deeper lines into his already weathered face.

He fumbled with his soaked shirt, extracting a small leather pouch from which he produced a business card, handing it to me with a resigned smile. "My name is Mason Thomas." He pronounced his name with an air of natural arrogance, a confidence stemming from a life steeped in privilege and responsibility. The name resonated with me immediately— Mason Thomas, a figure known in elite circles. As a scion of a noble lineage, he carried the weight of his heritage with quiet dignity. In the world of business, his reputation was one of steadfast reliability. His approach was conservative, averse to the siren call of speculative ventures that often ensnared others.

Sitting there, drenched and uncomfortable, I was eager to resolve whatever had drawn us into this unusual meeting. Mason continued to dab at his face, the rain still clinging to his skin. "It's my elder brother," he said, the words heavy with unspoken meaning.

"Why?" I prompted, seeking clarity.

His hesitation was palpable, as if he were wrestling with how much to reveal. I exchanged a knowing glance with Flora, silently communicating my skepticism. Her eyes met mine, a gentle reminder that we were already committed to this path.

Mason Thomas cleared his throat, attempting to explain. "Mr. Morris, my elder brother is older than me..."

I couldn't help but interject, "Isn't that obvious? If he's younger, he'd be your younger brother."

His expression, already harried by the rain, flushed with a mixture of embarrassment and urgency. "No, no, I mean much older. He's 38 years my senior. We're half-brothers. My father had me when he was 66."

The age gap between the brothers, a staggering 38 years, was unusual but not unheard of. Mason's tale of his father's late-life paternity was intriguing, yet ultimately irrelevant to my concerns. My impatience must have been evident, as Mason Thomas continued, "My brother is ninety-three years old this year."

I gestured for him to get to the point. "Tell me why he wants to see me. Be direct."

Mason Thomas hesitated, embarrassment coloring his expression. My gaze bore into him, compelling him to speak. Flustered, he finally managed, "He... is an astrologer."

Before I could respond, he added, "He... considers himself an astrologer."

"And?" I prompted, unimpressed.

With a resigned sigh, Mason Thomas pressed on, "Astrology... What he says, many people—ordinary people—can't easily understand. His age and health make it difficult. He's often incoherent..."

Finally grasping his meaning, I interjected, "You mean he's not coherent?"

Mason Thomas nodded earnestly, and I quipped, "Your explanation isn't exactly coherent either. Why does he want to see me?"

Clearly unused to such candid remarks, Mason Thomas bristled. "I don't know," he confessed, frustration tinging his voice. "He's insisted on meeting you for years. I ignored him because he seemed... unwell. But with his health failing and our chance encounter tonight..."

"Is he dying?" I asked bluntly.

"The doctors say it could be any day now. He's mostly unconscious," Mason Thomas admitted, his voice tinged with unease.

I exchanged a glance with Flora, who returned a wry smile. The prospect of meeting a dying astrologer was as perplexing as it was unusual, but curiosity pulled me forward.

Answers would come soon enough.

As the car continued its ascent, the rain lessened, the road gleaming under the headlights. We turned onto a hillside, revealing a sprawling mansion that loomed in the darkness, its silhouette vast and imposing. The eaves jutted like mythical creatures poised to take flight.

"What a grand house," I remarked, genuinely impressed.

"My father modeled it after the grandeur of a Georgian estate," Mason replied, his pride evident.

"If there are few people living here, it must take courage to reside in such a vast space," I mused, noting his agreement. Arriving at the entrance, the grandeur of the wrought-iron gates flanking the drive was striking. The driver honked, and the gates swung open, revealing a shadowed garden with countless pavilions and towers.

As we approached the main building, the rain ceased. Two uniformed servants descended the stone steps to open the car doors. Their eyes widened as they took in the sight of the wet Mason Thomas.

Flora and I followed him into the hall, where more servants gathered, their expressions a mix of curiosity and astonishment at our sodden state. A man who appeared to be the housekeeper rushed forward, addressing Mason Thomas with deference. "Master..."

Mason Thomas dismissed him with a wave. "Check if the eldest master is awake. Find dry clothes for our guests. Quickly!"

The housekeeper nodded, and though I was eager to meet the astrologer, the discomfort of my drenched clothing was undeniable. We were led to a room that blended Eastern and Western styles, reminiscent of affluent homes from a bygone era.

Our coats removed, the housekeeper returned with a bundle of clothes, retreating with a bow. I examined the garments, laughing at the antiquated style. The underwear was museum-worthy, while the outerwear—a long, tweed jacket—felt luxurious.

Flora's transformation was stunning. The dress she wore evoked the elegance of the Edwardian era, the lace and silk fabric having once adorned a lady of the house.

Rejoining Mason Thomas, he offered an apology. "I'm sorry. My brother never married, and my wife passed long ago. These are old clothes."

Flora smiled graciously. "They're exquisite. Such craftsmanship is rare today."

Mason Thomas led us through the dimly lit corridor, the high ceilings and muted lights giving the impression of a museum. At the end, a staircase spiraled upwards, and we ascended to the top floor, where the housekeeper met us with news. "The eldest master is invigorated by Mr. Morris's arrival and has taken ginseng soup."

Mason Thomas nodded, and I noted the layout was different here—no corridors, just two large doors adorned with a yin yang diagram that seemed almost mystical.
Several people awaited us, some appearing to be medical staff. They greeted Mason Thomas with deference. An elderly man spoke first. "The situation is grave—a temporary recovery before decline."

Mason Thomas acknowledged him, then looked to the others. One spoke up, "It might be, but his response to Mr. Morris's arrival is unprecedented."

Intrigued, I interrupted their deliberations. "Enough. I'm the one he wishes to see. Let me meet him."

The older man regarded me with skepticism. "Are you a doctor?"

I opted not to respond to the question, instead gesturing subtly to Mason Thomas. Taking the cue, he pushed open the door, and we stepped inside together. The sight that greeted me left me momentarily speechless.

The room was vast, occupying the entirety of the top floor. Bookshelves lined the walls, filled with thread-bound volumes, their spines like soldiers in formation. But what dominated the space was a massive bed, and on it lay a man who defied my expectations of a dying elder.

He was tall, almost imposing, even in repose. His skeletal frame was accentuated by the thinness of his body, making his presence both haunting and grand. His hair, short and white, stood stark against his pallor. His eyes, wide open, were unsettlingly bright, drawing my gaze upward.

Above the bed, the ceiling was a massive pane of glass, five meters on each side. Rain cascaded down its surface, creating an ever-shifting tapestry of patterns. The old man had designed his chamber with a singular purpose: to observe the heavens without obstruction.

Mason Thomas led Flora and me to the bedside. The astrologer turned his head slowly, fixing his luminous gaze on me. Despite his skeletal appearance, those eyes burned with an intensity that was almost otherworldly.

"Brother, Mr. Morris is here," announced Mason Thomas, his voice low and respectful.

The old man's gaze lingered on me, as if weighing my very essence. His voice, a raspy whisper, broke the silence. "Your father didn't come?"

His words caught me off guard. What could he possibly mean by that? Mason Thomas interjected, "Brother, this is Mr. Ash Morris."

The old man grunted, a sound like dry leaves rustling. "A little kid?"

I shook my head, a smile tugging at my lips despite the gravity of the situation. "Mr. Thomas, perhaps it's just that you've seen many more years than I."

With effort, the old man shifted, attempting to sit up. Mason Thomas rushed to his side, propping him up with a pillow. The astrologer's eyes turned skyward once more, though the only view was the rain-splattered glass.

I stood by, silent yet inwardly restless. Time seemed to slip away, each second precious, each moment one step closer to an end I feared was near. The weight of unspoken words hung in the air, and I willed him to speak before it was too late.

After a prolonged silence, marked only by the sound of rain, the old man finally found his voice. He coughed, a frail and lingering sound, then spoke with deliberate urgency. "Ash Morris, heed my words... I have no... time to repeat them! Listen, you must find them."

CHAPTER 2

THE DYING ASTROLOGER'S FINAL WORDS

I stood there, stunned, as the old man's words floated through the room, heavy with a thick accent. I grasped the language, yet its meaning slipped through my fingers like sand.

Before any questions could form on my lips, the old man erupted into a fervor, his frail body trembling as if possessed by some unseen force. He raised an unsteady hand, attempting to point, but age had stolen his strength, leaving only the ghost of a gesture. His voice, a raspy crescendo, filled the air: "Stop them! Stop... them..."Mason Thomas rushed to his side, seizing his hand, his voice a tether to reality: "Brother."The man's cries were a haunting echo, each word laced with a raw, hoarse urgency. His hands flailed, his body a symphony of involuntary motion, and I could almost hear the ancient creak of bones under the weight of his fervor.As Mason Thomas called his name, the old man's storm began to calm. Seizing the moment, I pressed forward, my mind racing against time: "Please, be more specific. Who are they? Where can I find them? Why must they be stopped?"The old man's gaze locked onto mine, his eyes a kaleidoscope of emotion, like flickering gems in the dim light. Under his scrutiny, a chill skittered down my spine, as though a centipede traced its path along my skin.

His gaze lingered, then shifted to Mason Thomas, who leaned in, his voice urgent: "Brother, what do you want me to do?"

The respect Mason Thomas held for his elder was palpable, a bond forged through decades of shared history.The old man's voice emerged once more, a guttural sound like gravel rolling in his throat. His finger, trembling with intensity, aimed at Mason Thomas, words sharp as daggers: "You... you little bastard, you lied to me. You brought a child here and claimed he was Ash Morris. You... you are a fool!"Mason Thomas bore the brunt of the old man's scolding, his face flushing with embarrassment. His eyes flicked towards me, filled with a mix of suspicion and frustration, as if I were a counterfeit, the unwitting catalyst of his reprimand.I couldn't help but laugh at the absurdity, anger and amusement mingling within me. "Yes," I chuckled, "I am not Ash Morris. I am merely pretending."

Shock washed over Mason Thomas's features. "You—" he began, but the old man interrupted, his voice cutting through the air like a knife. "Of course he's pretending. The real Mr. Morris wouldn't ask such foolish questions. Once I tell him, he would understand." With that, he reached out, tapping Mason 's head with a shaky hand. "You've been deceived... Go... Find the real Ash Morris... Time is slipping away."The old man's body swayed, and Mason, accustomed to his needs, helped him to lie back down. As he settled, his eyes remained open, wide and unblinking, staring into a reality only he could see.

Mason Thomas stood there, uncertain, as if navigating a landscape he no longer recognized. I was ready to leave, dismissing this encounter as mere theatrics, yet the old man's words had unsettled something deep within me.

I AM, of course, Ash Morris, yet the old man's dismissive certainty gnawed at my confidence. How could my questions be deemed foolish? His words had been a riddle wrapped in confusion.

Just then, Flora stepped in, her voice soothing in its sincerity. "Mr. Thomas, he likes to jest. He truly is Ash Morris. If you have instructions for him, please share."

There was something in her tone, something undeniably persuasive. Even the old man seemed swayed by her words, his gaze softening as he regarded her.

He turned back to me, a flicker of dissatisfaction still in his eyes, but he struggled to sit up once more. Mason hurried to support him, propping a pillow behind his back. The old man seemed rejuvenated, his eyes scanning me as if searching for hidden truths. I ignored his scrutiny, pulling a chair to sit facing him. His wrinkled brow furrowed at my audacity, yet he voiced no complaint, only a gruff snort. "Do you know they've been wreaking havoc for too long? What began as a mere disturbance has grown into chaos."

Even as he spoke with conviction, his words were a tapestry of incoherence. I glanced at Flora, whose own confusion mirrored mine. Mason offered only a weary smile.

I ceased my questions, knowing they might betray me as an imposter. Instead, I nodded, feigning understanding. "Yes, it truly is outrageous."

The old man sighed, finding solace in my agreement. "Indeed, the people suffer. What crime have they committed to endure such torment?"

I stifled a laugh, a mixture of disbelief and empathy welling within me. Here, in this room filled with shadows and secrets, the line between reality and performance blurred, leaving us all to question the truth.

The rain drummed relentlessly against the window, casting a symphony of shadows across the room. The old man, a relic of another era, seemed to find a kindred spirit as he spoke with an air of conspiratorial familiarity. "I had an old friend," he began, his voice a tapestry of nostalgia. "Before he passed, he urged me to find you. Though I gave him your name—a name of renown—it took Mason years to find you and bring me here."

Mason Thomas, his expression a mask of quiet indignation, interjected softly, "Brother!"

I couldn't help but smile, curiosity piqued. "Who facilitated this introduction?"

"Mr. Evans. Finley Evans," the old man replied, a name that hung in the air like an incantation.For a moment, I was taken aback, then filled with awe. Finley Evans was no ordinary figure. Though our paths had rarely crossed, his mastery of Chinese classical literature, medicine, divination, and astrology was legendary. His insights into metaphysics were unmatched, a beacon in a sea of the unknown.

Sensing an undercurrent of significance, I straightened in my seat, though a lingering unease tugged at my thoughts. "Indeed, Mr.Evans is someone I hold in the highest regard," I acknowledged.

The old man chuckled, his hand thoughtfully stroking his chin. " Finley Evans was but a youth when I taught him to read the stars."

I nodded, skepticism masked by politeness. With Finley Evans beyond this world, the old man had free rein over his tales, his words unchallenged by the constraints of proof.

He continued, a wistful reverie in his voice. "He began his celestial studies at thirteen, a full decade later than I—"

I swallowed, intending to let him continue uninterrupted, but the question slipped out. "Then you began at three?"

Without hesitation, he affirmed, "At three, the stars were my companions."

I muttered under my breath, "A prodigy before even Mozart composed," earning a sharp jab from Flora, who silently admonished my impertinence. Mason Thomas's face was a portrait of embarrassment.

The old man's gaze turned inward, his voice laden with the weight of nine decades of stargazing. ""For ninety years, I have witnessed the heavens' dance. Once, we were mere spectators, governed by them. But now, the world has grown wild. Something must be done. They must be stopped—"

I listened intently, realizing that no one alive could claim such an extensive understanding of the stars. His words demanded my attention, yet their meaning eluded me. Resigned, I reverted to a familiar tactic. "Indeed, we must act... but how?"

Inside, I cursed my inadequacy.

The old man's eyes, wide and unblinking, fixed on the rain-streaked glass above, where the sky's secrets lay hidden. "Someone must urge them to seek new horizons... anywhere but here... their games have brought us centuries of suffering."

He spoke in fits and starts, until a violent cough overtook him. I exchanged a glance with Mason Thomas, who deftly intervened. "Brother, you need rest. We'll continue another day."

To my surprise, the old man acquiesced. "Yes, tonight is not the night. The day after tomorrow...at midnight, yes, Mr. Morris, return then."

I offered a noncommittal smile, inwardly resolving to avoid his midnight musings.

Sensing my hesitance, Mason Thomas moved subtly, shielding my reaction from his brother. "Brother, it's time to rest."

The old man nodded, eyes still open as he lay back, an enduring enigma.

In a moment of curiosity, I asked, "Mr. Thomas, do you never close your eyes even when sleeping?"

His voice, heavy with sleep, answered, "No, not for ninety years."

I offered an "hmn," and the old man said again, "One can only see with eyes open."

I asked, "How can you see while you are in your dreams?"

A cryptic philosophy escaped his lips, "In dreams, one sees with the heart."

Surprised by such poetic wisdom from such an aged source, I thanked him for his insight.

The old man then remained silent, lying straight with his eyes wide open, looking extremely strange.

As we stepped away, Mason Thomas offered his apologies. "I'm sorry. I did warn you his words are not easily grasped by normal people."

With a wry smile, I conceded, "Not just difficult for the normal, but truly inscrutable for everyone."

Flora glanced at me, her silent disapproval evident.

Outside, the doctors clustered around Mason Thomas. He dismissed them, accompanying me to the living room where our rain-soaked garments awaited, freshly pressed.

Feeling a twinge of guilt, I turned to Mason Thomas. "Mr. Thomas, it's a pleasure meeting such diverse souls. Your brother is no exception."

He sighed, his invitation faltering on his lips. "The day after tomorrow, if you might..." His voice trailed off.

I clasped his shoulder reassuringly. "If my schedule permits, I'll be there."

His gratitude was palpable as he arranged our departure.

CHAPTER 3

FLORA'S INTERPRETATION

The drive home was thick with silence, interrupted only by the rhythmic swish of windshield wipers against the rain. I broke the quiet, turning to Flora. "Why the stern look earlier? Do you really think anyone can decipher the old man's ramblings?"

Flora shook her head, her gaze fixed on the road ahead. "I think we need to give his words more consideration. There's something there worth understanding."

A flash of irritation surged through me. "He could have been clearer. It's maddening to be left guessing."

After a pause, Flora spoke, her voice measured. "His message wasn't as cryptic as it seemed."

I raised an eyebrow, intrigued yet skeptical. "Enlighten me, because I found it incomprehensible."

"He often referred to 'they' in his speech," Flora explained. "It suggests a mysterious force. Given his lifelong study of astrology, it's conceivable he believes this force is tied to the stars."

I listened, her words weaving a pattern in my mind.

Flora continued, "Think about it—the influence he spoke of seems to be a celestial force affecting humanity's fate. He believes it's growing unchecked and needs to be halted."

I remained silent, absorbing her perspective.

Her interpretation was methodical, transforming the old man's disjointed musings into something coherent. Yet, I couldn't shake the feeling that he himself might not grasp the forces he feared.

Flora added, "He hoped you might counter this influence, having been introduced by Finley Evans."

I blinked, incredulous. "You think he expects me to ascend to the heavens and negotiate with the stars?"

Flora frowned at my flippancy, her disapproval palpable. I softened my tone with a smile. "People often ramble when they're near the end. Perhaps that's all it was."

Flora remained pensive, eventually admitting, "My explanation may lack clarity. I'm just as uncertain."

"You articulated it well," I assured her. "A mysterious power from the cosmos affecting Earth."

She nodded, then pondered, "If my theory holds, what kind of power could it be, and how might it influence us?"

Her question prompted serious reflection. With Flora watching intently, I lit a cigarette, the act helping to focus my thoughts, as I replayed the old man's cryptic dialogue in my mind.

"If such a force exists," I ventured, "perhaps it's a civilization with advanced science on some distant planet, controlling us through unknown means."

Flora's frown deepened. "That sounds like a plot from a mediocre sci-fi novel."

Had anyone else said it, I might have bristled. But coming from Flora, I merely blinked in mock protest. "You yourself speculated about a cosmic power affecting us."

She seemed to muse aloud, "Yes, but why assume this power stems from intelligent extraterrestrials?"

Her question baffled me. If a stellar force influences us, surely it must be more advanced. Yet Flora questioned this logic.

I muttered, "Then where else? A magical rock from another planet?"

Flora tilted her head, a sudden laugh escaping her lips. "Your words sometimes do make sense."

Her sudden agreement left me speechless. She had just dismissed my theory, yet now it held merit?

I waited for her to elaborate, but she offered nothing more. By the time we reached home, the topic seemed forgotten.

Inside, Flora didn't revisit the mystery of the old man's words, and neither did I. The evening held other distractions.

The phone rang as I stepped into the study. I answered, and Harlan Brown's voice, fraught with urgency, filled the room. "Thank God you're back."

Recognizing his voice, I nearly disconnected out of reflex, but his plea stopped me. "Don't hang up!"

Recalling how he had hosted us for months without complaint, I relented, slipping off my coat. "Alright, make it quick."

"I'm coming over," Harlan Brown declared, his tone brooking no argument.

I sighed, wondering what fresh intrigue awaited with his impending visit.

As the night deepened and shadows stretched long across the room, I found myself reluctant to entertain visitors. "It's hardly the time for social calls," I remarked, hoping to deter Harlan Brown from his impromptu visit. After all, it was late, and such unannounced visits seemed inappropriate.

But Harlan's enthusiasm on the other end of the line caught me off guard. "Ash," he

exclaimed, "you're studying astrology too, aren't you? I'm sure this is precisely the best moment for a visit, astrologically speaking."

His words left me momentarily speechless, unsure of how my casual remark had sparked such a response. "What on earth are you talking about?"

With a chuckle that hinted at some private amusement, Harlan replied, "The stars are aligned for visitors right now. It's an auspicious time for both hosts and guests. Gamblers in the southwest, however, are destined for ruin."

His talk of astrology piqued my interest, especially after the old man's cryptic musings earlier. Despite my initial reluctance, I couldn't help but be curious about what Harlan might say. Moreover, refusing him would likely result in persistent pestering.

Resigned, I sighed, "Fine, come over."

True to his word, Harlan arrived swiftly. In less than ten minutes, the doorbell rang with an insistence that bordered on obnoxious. As I moved to answer it, I called out, "It's

Harlan Brown. Brace yourself for whatever nonsense he's about to spout."

Flora's voice echoed from another room, urging me to answer the door. When I opened it, Harlan stepped inside, his grin wide and expectant.

Recalling his earlier proclamation about it being a "good time" for visits, I playfully delivered a light punch to his stomach, testing his theory. To my surprise, my fist met something solid beneath his shirt, eliciting a startled laugh from him as he revealed a hardcover book tucked under his clothes.

"Ash," he chortled, "I knew you'd try to catch me off guard. Preparedness is key when dealing with you!"

Though embarrassed by his foresight, I couldn't help but be amused. Yet, I feigned annoyance. "I am going to kick you now, and I doubt you've armored your legs."

Harlan's expression shifted to mock seriousness. "You won't," he declared.

I arched an eyebrow, intrigued by his confidence. "Why not? Care to wager?"

"Because," he replied with a grin, "the stars say it's an auspicious time for visiting friends. No unpleasantness will occur."

I considered kicking him just to defy his prediction but found it surprisingly difficult to muster the will. It was as if some unseen force indeed held sway over my actions.

Harlan noticed my hesitation and laughed triumphantly. "See? Even you can't defy the universe's laws."

Closing the door with a firm thud, I scoffed at his conclusions. "What universe's laws? You're spouting utter nonsense."

Despite my words, a small part of me wondered if perhaps, just perhaps, there was something more to his fantastical claims. After all, the night had already been filled with strange tales and inexplicable events.

CHAPTER 4

HARLAN'S STRANGE EXPERIENCE

Harlan Brown raised his hand with a solemn air. "A recent discovery of mine: the universe operates under laws shaped by the positions of countless planets, influencing everything on Earth."

He paused, waiting for the skepticism he knew would trigger his lengthy explanation. But I simply remained silent, feigning indifference to avoid encouraging his ramblings.

Undeterred, Harlan continued, "Take the moon, for instance. Its phases control the tides, and similarly, the movements of planets affect all life on Earth. If one could master this cosmic law..."

I cut him off with a teasing grin, "You could start a fortune-telling business or set up a stall."

Harlan stared at me, his voice rising in protest. "Ash, I can't believe you understand so little about astrology!"

In truth, I understood quite a bit. Astrology, with its broad scope, from predicting earthly events based on celestial movements to reading personal destinies, is deeply fascinating.It's grounded in the belief that Earth, as one of many planets, is inevitably influenced by the cosmos, and that life on Earth cannot escape the influence of other planets.

I knew astrology, but I doubted Harlan Brown had the same depth of understanding. So when he spoke, I merely smirked, refraining from debate.

After a moment, Harlan, disappointed by my lack of response, shifted his approach. "Even if you've studied astrology, you can't possibly know what I've recently discovered."

I gestured for him to join me in the study, where we settled into chairs. "Harlan, I'm not particularly interested in astrology tonight. I just spent an evening with a dying old man spouting starry nonsense..."

But before I could finish, Harlan's eyes widened in shock. "This... this old man's name is Theo Thomas?"

Surprised, I nodded. "I believe so. His brother is Mason Thomas."

Harlan snorted dismissively. "Mason Thomas's quite an arrogant pretender, always putting on an air."

I chuckled. "You're not his servant. Whatever airs he puts on don't affect you."

Yet Harlan's expression turned oddly sheepish, mingled with a peculiar pride. Hesitantly, he admitted, "I once worked as a servant for the Thomas family, serving Theo Thomas personally."

I was taken aback, incredulous yet amused. Harlan, with his affluent background and substantial inheritance, serving anyone seemed preposterous. It wasn't as if he was playing out some romantic pursuit disguised as a servant, like a literary hero.

"Truly," Harlan confirmed, "for about a year."

Eager for an explanation, I urged him, "Start from the beginning, but keep it succinct."

Just then, Flora entered, greeting Harlan with a wave. I called her over, eager to share the tale. "Harlan here claims he served in Mason Thomas's house for a year. Join us and hear his story—I suspect he was wooing the cook!"

Harlan retorted, "Don't be ridiculous. You know I've always been passionate about astrology. Everyone insisted there was only one true master: Theo Thomas."

Flora settled beside me, intrigued. Harlan, still slightly embarrassed, continued, "I sought Theo Thomas's guidance but was repeatedly turned away. Desperate, I saw a newspaper ad seeking servants with astrology knowledge to care for a difficult old man. Discovering it was the Thomas family hiring, I seized the chance."

I chuckled. "With your brilliant skills, they must have hired you on the spot."

Harlan detected my sarcasm and bristled, unsure how to respond. Flora intervened, "Mr. Brown, your dedication to learning is truly commendable."

Grateful for her support, Harlan nodded. "Thank you, truly."

He shot me a glare, which I pretended not to notice, content to let the evening unfold with its peculiar mix of cosmic theories and personal revelations.

Harlan Brown's tale unfolded like a forgotten legend, his eyes gleaming with the fervor of a man who had glimpsed the mysteries of the universe.

"As soon as I applied, the doors opened wide," Harlan began, his voice a whisper carried by the night breeze. "I became a servant, attending to the eldest master of the Thomas family. The job was as serene as the still waters of a hidden lake. Mr. Thomas spent his days either lost in the pages of his books or lying in bed, eyes tracing the celestial patterns above. His collection of tomes on astronomy and astrology was unparalleled, a treasure trove that the world could not match."I, too, had set foot in Theo Thomas's vast chamber. Although my opinions diverged from Harlan's in many respects, I could not deny the awe-inspiring library. I nodded in silent agreement.

Harlan's face lit up with delight. "He never forbade me from exploring his books. Whenever a question tugged at my mind, he would unravel its mystery. We shared a camaraderie, the old master and I, until one fateful day nearly ended it all."

I raised an eyebrow, the intrigue tangible. "What misstep did you take to provoke his ire?"

Harlan's expression turned aggrieved. "It wasn't my doing!" he protested. "At the head of his bed stood a small cabinet, lacquered black and adorned with gold—a guardian of secrets."

He paused, his gaze meeting mine as if to measure my understanding. I felt a twinge of embarrassment for not noticing this cabinet. But Flora, ever vigilant, interjected, "Indeed, there is such a cabinet, painted with the celestial Big Dipper. It bears an ancient lock—a Nine-Piece Chain Lock— a relic as enigmatic as the stars themselves."

Flora's words resonated with Harlan, who nodded fervently, his agreement almost comical in its eagerness—a habit perhaps honed during his year of servitude.He then turned to look at me, his gaze holding a challenge that sparked a flicker of annoyance within me. "Everyone knows," I retorted, "that such a lock is a labyrinth of complexity. Only a fool would be tempted by its riddle."

Yet, as Harlan recounted the tale of the cabinet and Thomas's wrath, I suspected that his curiosity had led him to test its lock. My intuition proved true as Harlan's cheeks flushed crimson, words failing him momentarily.

"I relish a challenge," he confessed, a hint of pride coloring his shame. "I turned to ancient calculations to decipher the lock. Whenever time permitted, I would attempt it in secret."

"Why such secrecy?" I probed.

Harlan's discomfort was palpable. "The first time... I meddled with it, the master rebuked me severely."

I sighed, understanding the futility of Theo's warning. Harlan's nature was irrepressible, and the master's admonition only fueled his resolve.

"It took me a month," Harlan recounted, eyes alight with the memory of triumph. "A month to breach the lock and reveal the inner sanctum—a smaller cabinet, guarded by twin chains of mystery. Just as despair threatened to claim me, the master, feigning sleep, caught me by surprise."

Laughter bubbled up within me at the image of Harlan caught red-handed, and even Flora couldn't suppress a chuckle.

Harlan's smile turned rueful, his tone laced with indignation. "The old man, with a strength belied by his years, seized my hair and bellowed like a wounded beast. The commotion drew a crowd, including Mason Thomas, who donned a mantle of authority to chastise me. But when I stood my ground, the master's anger dissipated, replaced by a strange respect. He dismissed the others and, after a contemplative silence, warned me once more—'The cabinet's secrets are not to be disturbed.'"

I couldn't help but ask, "Did you heed his warning?"

Harlan's eyes twinkled with mischief. "The locks proved too formidable. As the months passed and the master's health waned, I was dismissed, replaced by a retinue of doctors and nurses."

I mused, "An extra month's pay should be your due."

Harlan's playful punch was met with a deft block, our camaraderie undiminished. "Now is the auspicious moment for both hosts and guests. The time for friendship, not conflict," I chided.

Flora's laughter was a melody in the night. "Enough of this child's play. A year with the master, you must have gleaned much in the art of the stars?"

Harlan's demeanor shifted, gravity settling over him. "Indeed, I have affirmed a truth."

The air thickened with anticipation as Harlan prepared to share his revelation. "In the ancient tongue of our ancestors, all methods of divination are born of celestial motions. Every calculation mirrors the dance of the stars."

I pondered the weight of his words, "You call this a new discovery?"

Harlan nodded, his voice imbued with conviction. "Even the earliest divination classic, the 'Book of Changes,' is a celestial manuscript."

Though I had heard whispers of such theories, my knowledge was limited. I listened as Harlan continued, "For millennia, scholars have sought to unravel its mysteries, yet only by aligning it with the heavens can its wisdom be fully understood."

His enthusiasm was infectious. "For instance, 'a group of dragons without a head is auspicious.' What is the 'dragon' if not a constellation?"

I ventured, "It must be a formation of stars."

Harlan's hand clapped my shoulder, a gesture of shared enlightenment. "Precisely! When the stars align to form a dragon, yet its head is unseen, the day is blessed. All divination springs from the celestial ballet above."

In the quiet that followed, the night seemed alive with the whispers of ancient wisdom, the stars above bearing silent witness to secrets both known and yet to be discovered. The room seemed to hold its breath as I raised my hand, my voice calm yet firm. "I completely agree with you, Harlan, but I wouldn't call it a new discovery."

Harlan Brown's eyes blinked rapidly, his mind a whirl of thoughts eager to challenge. After a pause, he ventured, "Do you believe that the movements of the stars can influence all human activities on Earth?"

I frowned, grappling with the weight of his question. For centuries, some have held fast to the belief that celestial changes mirror the fates of mankind, shaping destinies and foretelling fortune and doom. This ancient wisdom, known as astrology, stretches back through the annals of history—where records abound of falling stars heralding the demise of generals in ancient China.

Astrology, with its enigmatic allure, suggests that a mere meteor streaking across the sky could seal a person's fate. Yet, offering a definitive answer eluded me, as the line between the mystical and the factual blurred.

Harlan's gaze bore into me, a challenge in his eyes. "Why, don't you always claim you can accept all the mysteries of the universe?"

I spread my hands, a gesture of openness. "Indeed, but such beliefs require more than mere imagination—they demand evidence."

Harlan seemed momentarily lost in his thoughts, my reasoning slipping past him like the wind. "If the stars can predict fortune and misfortune," he insisted, "then surely we can navigate life's perils and seize its blessings."

I snorted lightly, "In theory, yes. But only if the calculations are precise, foretelling exactly what events will unfold."

Harlan's smile was a bitter acknowledgment of his limitations. "Alas, my own research is shallow. Yet, Theo Thomas's mastery in this realm was nearly infallible."

I smiled softly, making no comment, while Harlan's demeanor turned serious, almost pleading. "Imagine the power to foresee the future, to know when and where disaster will strike. Such knowledge—"

I interrupted, my breath catching. "Knowing the future is a heavy burden."

Harlan's eyes widened as I continued, "In my experience, I've known two people with this gift. One, a beautiful girl, foresaw her own demise in a squalid place, her body left to decay. She sought desperately to prevent it, yet her fate unfolded exactly as she had foreseen."

"Terrible," Harlan murmured, the word a whisper of horror.

I spread my hands again. "The other was a brilliant scientist, aware he would die on the operating table. And so it was. He likened his life to reading an old newspaper—devoid of hope or surprise."

Harlan nodded slowly, recognition dawning. "You speak of Gina from the 'Heavenly Book' and George Lee from 'God of the Jungle.'"

I sighed, "Yes, two souls trapped by their own foresight."

Harlan waved his hands dismissively, his voice rising with conviction. "They brought it upon themselves. Gina knew her fate, yet chose only to stave off decay rather than change her destiny."

I considered his words carefully. "It's near impossible to alter a future you can predict."

Harlan pressed on, "Then why pursue preservation? Why not prevent death itself?"

Frustration tinged my reply. "When people are cornered, they often grasp at straws, seeking solace in futile endeavors."

Harlan persisted, "And Mr. George Lee—he willingly faced his fate on the operating table. It's illogical."

I groaned softly, "You try to defy fate?"

Harlan stood abruptly, his posture defiant, as if daring the universe itself. "Fate's greatest strength is its unpredictability. But if we can foresee its hand, why not change its course from the very roots?"

Flora and I exchanged glances, captivated by Harlan's fervor. His idealism, though naïve, held a certain charm.

Flora spoke gently, "Do you believe there's a way to change one's destiny or avert disaster?"

Harlan nodded vigorously, his belief unwavering.

I interjected, "Please, explain. How do you propose we alter what is destined to occur?"

Harlan waved his hands, a gesture betraying his own confusion. "First, let's establish a truth. Astrology divides into two schools. One claims terrestrial events are mirrored in the stars."

I nodded, "Yes, while the other asserts that celestial displays precede earthly occurrences."

Harlan leaned forward eagerly. "Which do you believe?"

I chuckled wryly, "I'm no astrologer. Who am I to judge which is correct?"

In that moment, the room held its breath again, the night alive with the echoes of ancient debates and the dreams of those who dared to challenge the stars.

The room seemed to pulse with an electric tension as Harlan Brown declared with unwavering conviction, "We must acknowledge that celestial phenomena precede worldly affairs. Only then can we alter the course of earthly events."

I leaned in, my voice steady. "Yes, but under your theory, to change worldly affairs, we must first alter the celestial phenomena themselves."

Harlan nodded with the enthusiasm of a man possessed by his ideas. "Precisely. If Mars shines too brightly, signaling a severe drought, then we must find a way to dim its brightness..."

I couldn't suppress a sharp laugh. "Do you even hear what you're suggesting?"

Harlan remained undeterred. "I'm merely illustrating how altering celestial events could change earthly outcomes."

I pressed on, "Your example is overly simplistic. Mars, the god of war, do you understand what you're implying?"

Harlan rolled his eyes, clearly unimpressed by my skepticism. "Of course I know. Is a lecture necessary?"

I continued, "Alright, when Mars unexpectedly brightens, it's called 'Mars Strong Illuminating' in astrology. This phenomenon often foretells drought."

"Yes," Harlan replied, a hint of impatience creeping into his voice. "Why repeat what's already known?"

I took a deep breath, "Your solution is to restore Mars to its usual brightness."

Harlan smirked, a mix of disdain and triumph in his eyes. "Finally, you grasp it."

I held back a mixture of anger and amusement. "And how, pray tell, do you propose to dim Mars's brightness, Mr. Brown?"

Harlan's eyes twinkled mischievously as he dismissed the logistics. "That's not my concern. Perhaps launch a rocket to Mars, trigger an explosion to dim it. Or maybe it brightens even more, who knows? The point is, to prevent drought, Mars must dim."

I resisted the urge to shake him. "Sure, and I have another method: distribute black glasses worldwide. With everyone wearing them, Mars seems dimmer, droughts vanish, and peace reigns."

Harlan's face flushed with indignation as he realized my sarcasm. "You're turning a groundbreaking idea into a jest!"

I sighed, the debate reaching its end. "There's no point in continuing this discussion."

Harlan's disappointment was palpable. "At least agree to take me along when you visit Theo Thomas."

I replied with a shrug, "The old man did invite me, but I doubt I'll go. He might not last long enough to see me again. If you can extend his life, perhaps with a rocket to divert a meteor, maybe he'll let you serve him longer."

Harlan's frustration boiled over, his face a vivid red. "Ash, you are the most insufferable man I've ever known!"

He stormed to the door, pausing to glare back, his anger battling with the urge to curse. To Flora, he barked, "I truly pity you."

With heavy steps, he descended the stairs, slamming the door behind him.

Flora's gaze turned to me, a mix of irritation and bemusement. I said:"What did you expect me to do? His ideas are absurd."

Flora pondered, "At least he proposed a theoretical approach to altering major world events."

I shrugged, "A theoretical approach that's utterly impractical is nothing but nonsense."

Flora chose not to argue, stretching languidly. That night, I immersed myself in astrology texts, seeking clarity amidst the chaos Harlan and Theo had stirred within me. Yet, the more I read, the more elusive the answers became. Eastern works were cryptic, Western ones shrouded in mystique. Still, one truth emerged—celestial movements, whether of neighboring planets or distant constellations, intricately weave the tapestry of earthly phenomena. As a mere speck in the cosmic dance, Earth is undeniably tethered to the vast celestial ballet.

BLACK GILDED BOX

The next day dawned with a flurry of tasks, and I resolved to set aside thoughts of astrology. The day unfolded in a blur of activity, and when I finally returned home, I was greeted by a sight that made me pause. A stack of astrology books had appeared on my desk, and Flora was deeply engrossed in them. I made a playful face at her before retreating to the solace of music.

By the third day, the sky had turned a sullen gray, and the afternoon brought with it a relentless downpour. The rain drummed incessantly against the windows, showing no sign of abating as the night crept in. At precisely 11 o'clock, the phone rang, its shrill tone cutting through the rain's melody. It was Mason Thomas, his voice hesitant yet urgent.

"Mr. Morris, my brother wishes to remind you of your midnight appointment."

I glanced out at the relentless torrent, the rain splattering against the window like a thousand tiny dancers. "Mr. Thomas wants me to stargaze tonight?" I replied, a hint of incredulity in my voice. "Surely we must reschedule. It's pouring near your place as well, isn't it?"

Mason's reply was immediate and assured, "The rain will cease shortly. By midnight, the skies will clear, and the stars will shine brightly."

His certainty left me momentarily speechless. "Have you consulted the observatory?"

Mason Thomas chuckled softly. "Observatory? Over the years, my brother's astronomical predictions have proven far more precise. They are unfailingly accurate."

Reluctant to dispute his conviction, I agreed. "Alright, if the skies clear, I'll be there."

Hanging up the phone, I turned to Flora, skepticism lacing my words. "What's with this old man? It's been raining all day, and the skies will clear just for his stargazing?"Flora smiled, a knowing glint in her eyes. "You've got it backward. He's invited us to stargaze because he knows the skies will clear."

I let the matter drop, handling a few calls and tasks until the clock read 11:30. The rain's symphony continued unabated, and I felt certain that our visit would be postponed. But then I saw Flora preparing to leave. I stared at her in disbelief until she calmly stated, "The rain has stopped."

Startled, I realized she was right. The sound of the rain had vanished. I stepped onto the balcony, and indeed, the downpour had ceased. The clouds were retreating like a theater curtain, revealing a waning moon obscured by wispy remnants. Within moments, the celestial stage was set, the stars and moon shining with renewed brilliance. Just as Mason Thomas had promised.

I quickly checked the time and, with a newfound urgency, prepared to leave. As I drove, I couldn't help but question Flora's confidence in the old man's prediction. "Why such faith in his foresight?"

Flora replied, "If a man has spent 70 or 80 years observing the sky, he'd better know when it'll rain or clear. Sometimes an old farmer's weather sense surpasses that of an observatory."

Despite my skepticism, the evidence was undeniable. Flora added, "While you were busy, I informed Harlan Brown."

I couldn't find a reason to object, so I remained silent.

Arriving at the Thomas estate, we were greeted by Mason Thomas. "You're right on time. My brother awaits." As we entered, Harlan Brown joined us, and Mason's surprise was apparent. I quickly explained, "This is Mr. Brown, a friend and a scholar of astrology. I'm sure your brother will enjoy meeting him."

Mason Thomas said nothing, simply nodding as he led us inside. Harlan Brown whispered his thanks to me, and I replied with a grin, "I hope the old man doesn't faint from shock at the sight of you."

Harlan stuck out his tongue playfully.

Theo Thomas's bedroom was as expansive as I remembered. My gaze was immediately drawn to the lacquered and gold-painted cabinet at the bed's head—a detail I'd overlooked before. Theo Thomas lay half-reclined, eyes fixed on the heavens through a vast glass ceiling. He acknowledged our presence without turning. "Ah, an old friend arrives. Harlan, it's been too long."

Harlan Brown, filled with respect, stepped forward. "Master, you deduced my presence?"

Theo gestured skyward. "Hercules and Kammuri, near to Capricorn, indicate that an uninvited guest arrives. Who else could it be except you?"

Harlan, following Theo's gesture, stared intently at the sky but seemed lost, unable to discern what the old master saw. I, too, was mystified, knowing only that Kammuri and Capricorn were star names.

Theo continued, "It's nearly midnight, Mr. Morris. Come, let me show you something."

His words were steeped in mystery, drawing me in. I moved closer, glancing at my watch—six minutes to midnight.

Flora joined me as we gazed upward. In that moment, Theo Thomas seemed ageless, his spirit vibrant as a child's, captivated by the celestial dance.

The night sky was a familiar canvas, accessible to all, yet Theo's passion painted it anew. The stars, ancient beyond measure, were there for all to see—a constant through the ages. I identified the constellations I knew and asked, "Mr. Thomas, what did you mean by Hercules and Kammuri being near Capricorn? Where are they?"

Theo waved dismissively. "Tiny stars, beyond ordinary sight."

I glanced back at him, searching for a telescope or similar tool, but found none. "How can you see what others can't?"

Theo's impatience was palpable. "Of course I can see them. Those stars reveal themselves to me because I understand them."

His cryptic answer left me puzzled, yet intrigued, as though on the brink of a

revelation just out of reach.

I glanced at him again, and he remained focused, gazing at the starry sky. But he could feel me looking back at him and shouted, his command echoing with urgency. "Look at the sky, not at me!" His vigor was surprising given his frail state. The unexpected fervor in his voice startled everyone, particularly his brother, Mason Thomas, who had last seen him in a much weaker condition.

Mason Thomas's concern was evident. "Brother, you..." he began, but Theo Thomas silenced him with a wave of his hand.

The old man's eyes sparkled with an ethereal light, an intensity that seemed to draw strength from the very stars he observed. I turned my gaze skyward, still puzzled by the cryptic directions. "Mr. Thomas, you said..."

I barely finished my thought when Mr. Thomas's voice, tinged with awe, broke the tension. "Look, look, it's coming, it's coming."

Caught off guard, Harlan Brown and I exchanged bewildered glances. The vast expanse above us seemed unchanged, a tapestry of stars as familiar as ever. Yet, the urgency in Theo Thomas's voice suggested a fleeting phenomenon, one that, if missed, might never be witnessed again.

Flora, ever the voice of reason amidst chaos, sought clarity. "Mr. Thomas, which part should we focus on?"

Theo Thomas's response was labored, each breath a battle. "Black Dragon... look... quickly."

His desperation was infectious, and though we couldn't see the significance, we felt compelled to comply. Mason Thomas, driven by concern, attempted to soothe his brother, reaching to rub his chest, only to be rebuffed with surprising strength.

The atmosphere immediately became tense. I didn't catch the point right away, as I always used modern astronomical terms, and I wasn't very familiar with ancient eastern astronomical terms. Theo Thomas's sudden urgency might have been due to the fleeting changes in astrology, which made me very nervous. For a moment, I couldn't remember which part he wanted me to see. Looking at Harlan Brown, I saw his focused expression, but also full of uncertainty.

The atmosphere crackled with tension, a shared understanding that the changes were ephemeral. I racked my brain, recalling the ancient terms that had slipped my mind. Flora's whisper came like a guiding star, "Seven Stars in the East."

I nodded, turning my attention eastward. The Black Dragon, was an ancient Chinese astronomical term—a celestial formation symbolized by seven stars. It spanned a section of the sky that included modern constellations such as Virgo, Scorpio, Libra, and Sagittarius.

In ancient China, astronomers divided the observable constellations into twenty-eight groups, with each group of seven forming the image of an animal. They imagined several stars in the east as a dragon and called it the Black Dragon. The other three groups of stars among the Four Symbols are the Vermilion Bird, the White Tiger, and the God of Creation.

The Black Dragon, also known as the Eastern Seven Stars, includes the Jiao Star, Kang Star, Di Star, Fang Star, Xin Star, Wei Star, and Ji Star. In total, there are more than thirty visible stars, including many stars in the modern constellations of Virgo, Scorpio, Libra, and Sagittarius, arranged in the southeast of the vast starry sky.

These stars were meant to hold a secret visible only to Theo Thomas's trained eye.

I strained to see what he saw, my eyes tracing the familiar path of the constellations. The highest star, Jiao—or Spica in modern terms—was easily identifiable, a bright beacon in the Virgo constellation.It's number is "one".

(Disclaimer: In this story, many star names will be mentioned. In modern astronomy, star names are represented by Greek letters, which can be difficult to typeset and read. Therefore, all star names will be replaced with corresponding numbers. There are twenty-four Greek letters, and the first letter will be considered as "one," and so on.)

Guided by Flora's reminder, I found Jiao, the dragon's head, known in modern terms as Spica, the brightest star in Virgo. This first-magnitude star was easily identifiable, forming an equilateral triangle with other prominent stars.

Focused on Jiao, I saw nothing out of the ordinary. I prepared to search for other stars in the Black Dragon when Mason Thomas's urgent cry drew my attention. "Doctor, come quickly!"

His plea pulled me from my celestial musings. I glanced down, noticing the palpable tension in the room. Theo's face was a mask of intensity, his hands gesturing wildly, sweat streaming down his furrowed brow. His condition was alarming, and Mason's call for medical assistance seemed prudent.

As the door swung open, admitting a team of medical professionals, Theo's voice rose to a shrill crescendo. "Everyone else, out! Ash, you must see this, quickly!"His finger pointed skyward, trembling with urgency.

Flora, sensing the gravity of the moment, gently tugged my sleeve and reassured, "Yes, Mr. Thomas, he is watching."

I exchanged a glance with Flora, both of us aware that the mystery of the Black Dragon eluded us.

The doctors hesitated, unsure of how to proceed, while Mason Thomas stood frozen, caught between duty and disbelief.

Theo's voice cut through the confusion, a keening wail. "Out, all of you, you don't understand... Look, focus on Ji Star Four, Ji Star..."

His breath came in rapid bursts, each word laden with a sense of foreboding. I quickly identified Ji Star Four, a star in Sagittarius, near the Lagoon Nebula. Yet, despite the old man's insistence, it appeared unremarkable—just another point of light in the vastness above.

Harlan Brown, equally perplexed, inquired, "Master, what's wrong with Ji Star Four?"

Theo Thomas's reply was sharp, imbued with a cryptic significance. "Starlight, the starlight of Ji Four points east, and another starlight in Wei Star Seven echoes it..."

In a move that defied his frailty, Theo Thomas suddenly sprang to his feet on the bed, his figure silhouetted against the starry backdrop.

In the dimly lit room, this unexpected motion sent a ripple of fear through the small gathering. The old man, precariously balanced on the mattress, swayed like a leaf in the wind. Mason Thomas, initially frozen by shock, suddenly sprang into action, a cry tearing from his throat, "Brother!"

With urgency, he lunged forward, wrapping his arms around the old man's legs to anchor him. Theo Thomas stood above, his eyes wide, his breath ragged, his face a mask of bewilderment and dread. His hands reached upwards, palms facing the heavens, as if he were Atlas himself, straining under an invisible weight.

Flora, Harlan Brown, and I exchanged bewildered glances, paralyzed by uncertainty. The room was silent, save for Theo Thomas's labored breathing. Just as I steeled myself to intervene, Theo Thomas's voice pierced the air, "Do you see it? Each of the seven eastern constellations holds a star glowing with starlight."

Flora furrowed his brow, while Harlan Brown's mouth hung agape. Their eyes, like mine, turned skyward, yet comprehension eluded us. The night sky twinkled with countless stars, their distant light dancing in the darkness. What was this starlight Theo Thomas spoke of? Was it a faint glimmer, or something else entirely? Among the myriad stars in the eastern constellations, nothing seemed amiss.

Theo Thomas's voice rose again, trembling with urgency, "Look! The seven starlights! It's as I feared. The day has come when the seven starlights merge into one. A catastrophe is upon us."

His cries grew hoarse, the desperation in his words wrapping around us like a suffocating mist. Mason Thomas clung to his brother, tears threatening to spill from his eyes, "Brother, please, lie down. Lie down first."

In the suspenseful silence that followed, the weight of Theo Thomas's prophecy hung heavy, an enigma wrapped in the ancient tapestry of stars, science, and the ominous whisper of fate.

In an unexpected surge of strength, the old man, Theo Thomas, let out a sharp yell, his foot striking out with surprising force to send Mason Thomas sprawling backward. His arms still strained upwards, as if holding back the sky itself, his voice a ragged plea, "Don't let them succeed, don't... stop them..."

Desperation clawed at my voice as I asked, "What are they trying to do? Who are they?"

Theo Thomas's voice rasped through the air, each word a struggle, "They seek to unleash disaster... a calamity from the east. Ash, you must stop them... There have been only three times in history when the seven stars shone their starlights in unison... This is the third. Ash, you must stop them... You..."

His voice faded into a strained whisper, and as the room plunged into an eerie silence, Mason Thomas, undeterred by the kick, rushed back to his brother's side, clutching his legs once more.

Suddenly, the old man's voice ceased entirely, leaving an unsettling quiet that pressed heavily upon us. The silence was unnatural, stifling. Flora and I both gasped, the oppressive stillness amplifying our unease. Even in silence, Theo Thomas's labored breathing should have filled the air, but instead, there was nothing.

Startled, I turned to Theo Thomas, his body frozen in that same upward-reaching stance, eyes wide, mouth slightly ajar. A chill ran through me as I met his gaze. Once vibrant and enigmatic, his eyes now held a dullness, as though a thin film had settled over them.

Realization struck hard: Theo Thomas was dead. Yet, Mason Thomas, oblivious to this truth, clung desperately to his brother's legs. I breathed a heavy sigh, stepping forward to rest a hand on Mason Thomas's shoulder, "Help him lie down. He's gone."

Shock registered on Mason Thomas's face as he released his grip, his brother's arms falling limply, his body collapsing back, eyes still open, unseeing. Mason Thomas flailed, lost in his grief, the bond with his brother unbroken even in death.

Though Theo Thomas had lived over ninety years, his passing was a profound blow to Mason Thomas, leaving him adrift in sorrow. The weight of unspoken words and unfulfilled warnings hung over us, a reminder of the mystery and menace that loomed on the horizon.

As the medical team approached the bedside, their presence felt almost redundant. Flora and I exchanged a knowing glance; we were certain of the inevitable—Theo Thomas was beyond saving.

Mason Thomas's grief erupted at last, his pleas desperate and raw. "Hurry up and save him, hurry up and save him... He fainted... Hurry up and give him an injection, hurry up!"

The futility of his hope drew words from my lips, "Mr. Thomas, your brother is dead."

Mason Thomas's reaction was instantaneous and fierce, his finger jabbing the air as he shouted, "Get out, get out. Who said he was dead? You shouldn't have come at all, you... you... get out!"

Though anger simmered within me, I held my tongue. It wasn't my place to confront someone in the throes of such a staggering loss. Flora, sensing my agitation, gently tugged at my arm, "We should go."

I turned on my heel, Harlan Brown trailing behind, and as we reached the door, frustration spilled over. "It's absurd," I snapped to Flora. "I came to hear the ramblings of an old madman and now I'm furious, with nowhere to vent."

Harlan Brown, unfazed by the tension, offered his interpretation with a solemnity that bordered on reverence. "What the master spoke of was the mysterious will of Heaven. He revealed the divine plan and thus met his end immediately."

I shot him a skeptical look. "What are you talking about? What divine plan?"

He pointed skyward, conviction in his voice. "Theo Thomas saw the stars shift and foresaw disaster in the east.

He trusted you, Ash, believed only you could avert this catastrophe. But you dismissed him as a madman."

A laugh escaped me, edged with bitterness. "Yes, indeed. I was flattered. Perhaps he should have asked you to prevent this disaster."

Harlan Brown's eyes narrowed at my sarcasm, a silent challenge. I continued, "Why don't you get a powerful space rocket, strap yourself in, and shoot up to the stars? Dispel the abnormal starlights of Ji Star Four, Xin Star Three, and Fang Star Two. Without them, disaster averted, right?"

His face flushed with indignation. "You don't understand anything at all."

I raised my hands, conceding, "Yes, I admit it."

Flora sighed, her voice weary. "Let's move on. There's no point in arguing now. Get in the car."

With the weight of unspoken words and unresolved mysteries hanging between us, we stepped into the night, leaving behind the echoes of prophecy and the chill of fate's inexorable march.

As we left, the three of us had originally arrived in my car, but now Harlan Brown's temper flared, and he stormed off, his voice trailing behind him, "I don't ride with people who know nothing."

I couldn't resist a bit of teasing. "Watch out, walking alone at night. You might run into seven people in black clothes."

He paused, turning back with a puzzled look. "What seven people in black clothes?"

I chuckled, unable to help myself. "The substitutes for the Seven Stars of the East. It's also called the Black Dragon. Naturally, they'd wear black. Perhaps their faces are black too."

With a frustrated cry, Harlan Brown marched off into the night. I climbed into the driver's seat, still chuckling, while Flora settled quietly beside me, saying nothing.

We both knew why I delayed driving off—to give Harlan Brown a head start before catching up to offer him a ride again. The silence between us was companionable, filled with shared understanding.

Soon, the wail of sirens broke the quiet. An ambulance pulled up, lights flashing, a testament to Mason Thomas's refusal to accept his brother's demise.

I started the car, moving slowly down the road. Flora finally broke the silence. "I doubt Harlan Brown will get back in the car."

I sighed, "He's quite a character, interesting even, but too peculiar and lacking humor."

Flora merely hummed in response. I prodded gently, "Any objections?"

She mused, "Well, if someone else joked like that about you, how would you react?"

I waved off the thought, "I wouldn't give anyone the chance to mock me like that, so there's no use speculating."

Flora sighed thoughtfully, "Mr. Thomas's words might not be mere ramblings. He had his own unique insights from all those years of stargazing."

I held my tongue. If it had been anyone else, I might have said, "Even if he's right about the stars predicting disaster, what can we do, bound to this earth?"

But with Flora, I simply let the silence stretch, until she turned my words back on me, "Any objections?"

I laughed, about to reply, when something caught my eye. There, perched on a large roadside rock, was Harlan Brown. He stood with arms raised, palms skyward, mirroring Theo Thomas's eerie posture from earlier.

I stopped the car abruptly, rolling down the window. Once open, I heard him, his voice echoing Theo Thomas's last words, "Don't let them succeed. Stop them!"

A chill ran down my spine, the night's air thick with the weight of prophecy and uncertainty, as if the stars themselves were watching, waiting.

The night air was crisp as I leaned out of the car window, calling into the shadowy expanse, "Harlan Brown, enough of these theatrics. Get in the car."

Harlan Brown turned, a look of genuine surprise etched on his face. "Ash, have I ever asked anything of you?"

I let out a derisive laugh. "More times than I can count."

His voice wavered, urgency lacing his words. "Yes, I've asked you for countless favors, yet you've never obliged. But now, I beg you, step out of the car and stand beside me."

His stance was odd, an unyielding determination in his eyes. Despite my reluctance, the earnestness in his plea tugged at my conscience. Resignedly, I exchanged a glance with Flora, shrugged, and exited the vehicle. I clambered onto the large rock where Harlan Brown stood, joining him in his peculiar vigil.

Still in that strange pose, Harlan Brown whispered, "Do you know what I'm doing? I'm testing to see if Theo Thomas was silenced by some mysterious force for revealing a secret. If my suspicions are correct, I should feel that force now."

I sighed, a deep, genuine breath of exasperation. "I suggest you stop this nonsense. If your little experiment succeeds, you'll end up a victim of the same mysterious power from the Seven Stars of the East."

My words were flimsy at best, but Harlan Brown's resolve was unwavering. "What's my life worth if it proves the truth? If I'm right, you'll have no choice but to act to avert this catastrophe."

His bravado was both laughable and perplexing. Though I never doubted his grand heart, his blind faith in Theo Thomas's ominous warnings was beyond me.

"How long do you intend to stay like this?" I inquired, impatience creeping into my voice.

Harlan Brown sighed, "I don't know. I've been here a while, yet I feel nothing."

Suddenly, he called out, "Ash!"

Startled, I quickly responded, "Don't expect me to join your odd experiment."

He sighed once more. I preemptively cut off his request, leaving him no room to speak. After a moment, he said, "Ash, you know astrology speaks in its own language."

I chuckled, "We can dissect that in the car."

Convincing Harlan Brown to abandon his quest was no small feat. I figured if I could get him into the car and drive him home, his eccentricities would be his own problem. Leaving him on this roadside was not an option.

But unexpectedly, Harlan Brown shook his head with a stubborn grin. "No, we discuss it now. The language of astrology is enigmatic, yet it can be translated. For instance, 'fate' might describe a star's unique influence on a person."

I murmured an acknowledgment, contemplating whether knocking him out would be the quickest solution.

Just then, Flora joined us, silhouetted against the night sky.

Harlan Brown continued, "You must accept that human thoughts and actions are affected by countless celestial bodies. If you can't acknowledge astrology's foundation, there's nothing more to discuss."

His conviction was unyielding, and beneath the stars, I realized this was just the beginning of another bewildering journey.

I seized the moment to interject, "I don't buy it, Harlan. Let's end this discussion."

Harlan Brown's expression took on a fervent glow, like a martyr defending his cause. "No, Ash, deep down you understand astrology's essence. The universe is teeming with stars, each radiating unique energy towards Earth, influencing those sensitive enough to feel it."

I let out another sigh, choosing silence, but Flora stepped in to elucidate Harlan Brown's point. "In ancient terms, someone uniquely touched by a star's energy was said to embody that star on Earth."

Harlan Brown beamed, his enthusiasm palpable. "Exactly! A person gifted with extraordinary literary talent, influenced by a star, would be seen as the embodiment of Wenquxing (Megrez). Conversely, someone driven to malevolence might be deemed an evil star's earthly form."

All I could muster was another weary sigh. My voice lacked the fervor that animated Harlan Brown. "Sure, like the 108 Liangshan heroes, each aligned with celestial phenomena."

Harlan Brown's gaze was solemn. "I believe the world's exceptional individuals are all aligned with the cosmos, guided by stellar influences. Ordinary folk remain ordinary because they lack this celestial touch."

His words left me in awe, not of their truth, but of the sheer imagination they revealed. He had woven ancient folklore with cosmic mystery, suggesting that a star's force could shape human destiny—a theory both audacious and intriguing.

Nodding, I conceded, "It's an interesting theory."

Harlan Brown's face lit up with gratitude. "Thank you."

With that, he fell silent. Curious, I probed further, "You've taken me on quite the philosophical journey. What's your point?"

After a brief pause, Harlan Brown confessed, "I've stood here with this gesture, speaking like this, yet I feel nothing. Theo Thomas keeps pointing you towards these cosmic anomalies. He must believe you're..."

I cut him off, raising my voice. "I have no idea what star I hail from. Perhaps I'm just from an unlucky one."

I meant it as a jest about my friendship with Harlan Brown, but he took it seriously, "What do you mean? Are you saying Mrs. Morris isn't worthy of you? So you accept your fate as an unlucky star."

His earnestness amused me. "You're an extraordinary person, Ash. I'm convinced you're influenced by some celestial body."

As I descended from the rock, my patience waning, I quipped, "When you identify that star, let me know. Perhaps when it falls, you'll know I'm gone."

With that, I stepped away, leaving Harlan Brown in his world of celestial dreams, while I returned to reality, pondering the mysteries of the universe and their peculiar hold on us.

Harlan Brown mused, "In life, few can discern which star influences them. The emperor, for instance, is often under the sway of the Purple Star."

I leapt from the rock, feeling the weight of Harlan Brown's disappointment. "I had hoped that by mimicking my posture and words, you might sense the impending cosmic catastrophe threatening the East."

I sighed, a familiar exasperation. "I appreciate your faith in me, but I'm no celestial envoy. I'm just an ordinary person, and I've seen no signs or omens."

Harlan Brown's voice dropped, laden with frustration. "Truth be told, I've seen nothing myself. But Theo Thomas spoke of seven starlights aligning in the eastern constellations."

"Theo Thomas also claimed he could sense the stars with his mind while sleeping with his eyes open," I retorted, casting doubt on the reliability of the old man's words.

Yet Harlan Brown remained resolute. "If star influence is a form of mysterious radiation, then perhaps sensing with the mind is indeed more effective than mere observation."

I could no longer contain my irritation and shouted,"Harlan Brown, are you getting in the car or not?"

He shook his head defiantly. Flora gave me a knowing look, urging me to humor him. Rarely did I lose my patience with Flora, but now I snapped, "You want me to indulge this madness too?"

Flora sighed softly. "No, I just think that while Theo Thomas's words are cryptic, they hint at a disaster that might be preventable—by you."

I smiled bitterly at the notion that I could unravel the cosmos' mysteries. How could I, a mere mortal, contend with celestial forces? The stars were light-years away, beyond human reach or comprehension.

But Flora persisted gently. "Mr. Brown's persistence has merit. You won't lose anything by trying."

I chuckled, albeit wryly. "Your suggestion shows your skepticism. If you truly believed I could channel some heavenly insight or intercept cosmic radiation, you wouldn't ask me to try on a whim. What if I'm silenced for uncovering a secret?"

Flora looked torn. "I don't know. My thoughts are conflicted, but I think it's worth a shot."

Her eyes were wide, silently pleading. I pondered her unexpected insistence. Flora wasn't one to chase whims. Perhaps, as she said, her thoughts were muddled, and she sought clarity by testing an improbable theory.

Even if Harlan Brown had dropped to his knees and pleaded with me, I would have dismissed such nonsense without hesitation. But under the influence of Flora's gentle, imploring gaze, I sighed and reluctantly surrendered my resolve.

With a shake of my head, I climbed back onto the large rock. It had been ages since I'd indulged in anything so absurd. Mimicking Harlan Brown, I raised my hands to the heavens, my eyes wide and fixed on the constellations above. Then, with more theatrics than conviction, I yelled, "Don't let them succeed. Stop them."

Harlan Brown echoed my cries, and I could only imagine the bewilderment of any passerby who happened upon our spectacle—a scene befitting an escape from the local asylum.

After a few shouts, I deemed Flora's curiosity satisfied and prepared to descend. But then, something stopped me cold. My mouth hung open, words caught in my throat.

In the southern sky, amidst the Seven Eastern Constellations, a few stars — distant and seemingly ordinary—suddenly flared with an eerie light. Seven beams of vibrant colors, as thin as gossamer threads, shot out, converging from various directions to a singular point.

The convergence point was a void, starless and dark. But as the beams united, a starburst erupted—a vivid, scarlet bloom against the infinite black, like a drop of blood on velvet. The spectacle, though fleeting, seared itself into my mind, leaving a momentary afterimage as the stars vanished into the night.

Describing the event demands a plethora of adjectives, but in reality, it transpired in less than a heartbeat.

The first thing I did was glance at Harlan Brown. His face was still upturned, oblivious, his expression unchanged. Had I truly witnessed a celestial marvel? Why was I alone in this vision? Was it a hidden ability, or merely a trick of the mind?

The thought sent shivers through me. The night sky had returned to its unremarkable state, and I remained rooted in place, my only movement the turn of my head. Flora's voice broke through my reverie, tinged with urgency. "What did you see?"

For a moment, I hesitated, my voice emerging raspy and unsure. "Nothing. I didn't see anything."

I knew, though, that after years of marriage, Flora could detect my lie. Avoiding her gaze, I lowered my hands and called out, "Harlan Brown! Experiment's over. Let's get back in the car."

Harlan Brown's shoulders slumped as he too lowered his arms. He sighed, a murmur of disbelief escaping him. "It doesn't make sense. I trust Theo Thomas's words. For a year, I watched him predict events from the stars without fail."

Curiosity piqued, I asked, "Can you give me an example?"

Harlan Brown's eyes lit up, recounting, "Once, he noted that the Pleiades and the Tianhuang star were dim, predicting disaster for a Western leader. The next day, news broke of the U.S. president being attacked. Another time, he foresaw an earthquake when Tianxuan was disturbed by an alien star. And it happened."

I frowned, skeptical. "If you're referring to that famous earthquake, the timing doesn't match. You weren't with the Thomas family then."

Harlan Brown nodded earnestly. "True, but that day, Theo Thomas was in high spirits and shared a record with me, showing prior knowledge of the earthquake. Hundreds of thousands perished."

I said nothing more, descending from the rock. Harlan Brown followed, still muttering. I ignored him as we got into the car, the silence thick with my tangled thoughts. He wanted to continue our discussion back home but refrained, sensing my distraction. As we parted, he said, "Let's stay in touch. Whoever learns anything first will inform the other, agreed?"

I nodded. After Harlan Brown left, Flora quietly remarked, "It's unfair to Harlan Brown."

I sighed, rubbing my temples. "I know, but things are bizarre. I need to clear my head."

Flora didn't press for details. I reached out, gently brushing her hair. As we arrived home, I promised, "I'll explain once we're inside."

Flora nodded but pointed towards our door. "Look, we have guests."

A large black RV was parked outside, its driver in uniform, the seats covered in pristine white cloth. Familiarity crept over me; it was the same RV I'd boarded in the rain, the night I met Theo Thomas.

As I stepped out of the car, I mused, "Mason Thomas? Impossible. His brother just passed; why would he come here?"

Flora shared my puzzlement. I hurried to the door, where Wilson, our old servant, was arguing, "I don't know when Mr. Morris will return. Wait if you must, or leave the box and go."

Wilson's irritation suggested the visitor had been less than courteous. I strode into the living room. "I'm back···"

I stopped short, stunned. There, red-faced and fuming, was Mason Thomas himself.

His presence was a shock. He'd been the one to drive me away from the Thomas family, and now he was here. Why?

Mason Thomas glared at Wilson, who turned away defiantly. Pointing to a lacquered box on the floor, he snapped, "My brother's will instructed that I give you this box personally. No one else. Now it's done, I'm leaving."

With that, he turned to go.

The box was unmistakable, the same one from Theo Thomas's bedside, still secured with its nine-piece chain lock. The situation felt abrupt, riddled with unanswered questions.

Less than an hour since Theo Thomas's death, and already Mason Thomas had accessed his brother's will? Suspicious, I remarked, "You didn't waste any time reading your brother's will, did you?"

Mason Thomas bristled, "What nonsense are you spouting?"

I pointed at the box, challenging, "You claim this is Mr. Thomas's last will. How could you know that without reading it?"

My confidence seemed to incense Mason Thomas further. "Bullsh — " he began, but caught himself, remembering his status, and stopped short of finishing the curse.

I maintained my gaze, unwavering, awaiting his response. He swallowed hard, then blurted, "My brother told me on his deathbed."

His words widened my eyes in disbelief. How could someone lie so blatantly? I had been there when his brother died. The old man's final words were a plea to me, "Ash, you must stop them," before his breath ceased.

I shot back, "What are you talking about? I was present when Mr. Thomas passed. I heard his last words."

Mason Thomas suddenly charged toward me, patience frayed. He finally spat out, "You're talking nonsense! You said he was dead, but he wasn't. The old man only just passed out."

His assertion left me momentarily speechless. Flora interjected, "Mr. Thomas, are you saying that after we left, Mr. Theo...he..."

Mason Thomas grumbled, "I don't have time for your nonsense, but my brother valued you. He woke, sat up, and instructed me to give you this box."

I was genuinely taken aback. I could distinguish between life and death, and if I had been mistaken, I'd be better off knocking sense into myself with a brick.

Yet, Mason Thomas had no apparent reason to deceive me. I pressed, "Mr. Thomas, there's no need to rush. Please, detail what happened."

Flora added, "Yes, it'll only take a few minutes. Mr. Theo Thomas entrusted him with a task. Understanding every detail is crucial to honoring his wishes."

Maybe it was Flora's earnest plea that softened Mason Thomas's demeanor. He snorted, his anger dimming slightly. "After you left, those doctors declared him dead..."

I wanted to interject, "He really was dead," but held my tongue.

Mason Thomas's voice was thick with emotion., "I called for an ambulance and shook him repeatedly, trying to rouse him."he said, his voice catching. I could picture the scene— Mason Thomas, distraught, trying desperately to revive his elder brother whom he deeply revered. It was a poignant image.

But the reality was stark—the dead cannot be revived by mere shaking. If it were that simple, death would hold no sway over us.

Mason Thomas continued, voice trembling. "I shook him, and then he just sat up, straight as an arrow. The doctors, they panicked, stumbling over themselves. Shameless fools."

I offered a faint smile. The notion of a corpse suddenly reviving was unsettling, stirring primal fears. No wonder the doctors, who had pronounced him dead, were unnerved. Mason Thomas's disdain for them seemed misplaced, yet understandable in his grief.

Without waiting for my response, he went on, "He pointed to the box and said, 'Mason, give this box to Ash Morris immediately. Personally. Don't leave until he has it. Not a moment's delay.' I was elated to see him awake and agreed right away. Then the ambulance came, but after those words, he collapsed again, and this time... he was truly gone. No amount of calling or shaking could bring him back."

Mason Thomas's despair was palpable. He paused, then added, " Remembering his last words, I knew I couldn't delay. I had to deliver this box to you first, but you weren't here, and your housekeeper was..."

Hurriedly, I interjected, "I'm truly sorry." Mason Thomas sighed heavily, "I must go. My brother's death leaves so much to handle."

We escorted him to the door. "What's in the box?" I asked.

Mason Thomas shook his head. "I haven't a clue. It's yours now, whatever's inside. You have full authority over it."

With that, he hastened to his car, urging the driver onward. The vehicle screeched away, vanishing from sight.

Once alone, I remarked, "Theo wasn't unconscious when we left—he was dead."

Flora nodded thoughtfully. "Yes, he was gone while standing there."

I spread my hands in disbelief. "It's baffling. How does a deceased person return just to deliver a message about a box?"

Flora didn't answer immediately. He entered the house, standing by the mysterious box, running his fingers along its surface, lost in thought.

The box was exquisite, reminiscent of those now replicated for Western decoration, yet once a staple in Chinese households. The black lacquer gleamed, and the gold-painted Big Dipper and swirling clouds retained their vividness.

As I fiddled with the intricate nine-ring lock, Flora mused, "There are cases of people reviving after clinical death."

I nodded, recalling, "Yes, accounts exist. An American doctor documented many such occurrences in a book."

"So," Flora pondered, "while Theo Thomas's revival isn't unheard of, why was this box so crucial to him?"

I shrugged, "We'll find out once we open it."

The mystery of the box loomed large, promising revelations or, perhaps, more questions. As we prepared to unlock its secrets, the air was thick with anticipation and the weight of Theo Thomas's enigmatic final act.

As I spoke, my fingers danced over the intricate lock, a nine-link puzzle that seemed to defy logic and time. Its complexity was maddening, a labyrinth of metal that demanded precision and patience. Only those familiar with its secrets could hope to unlock its mysteries.

Harlan Brown had conquered this challenge before, revealing yet another layer of enigma — a smaller box, shrouded in its own mystery, secured by a miniature twin of the original lock.

The lock's appearance was deceiving, its fragility a facade. I resolved to bypass the ritual of unlocking, opting instead for brute force—the most straightforward path to revelation.

Flora's hand caught mine, her eyes a silent plea. "This is the quickest way," I argued, urgency in my voice.

She nodded, but her words were a gentle warning. "Yes, but Mr. Thomas would see it as a betrayal of trust."

I chuckled, dismissing the ghost of the past. "He's gone, Darling. Even after his miraculous return, he won't rise again."

Her gaze was steady. "I just don't want anyone thinking we're incapable of solving such a puzzle."

"Who says it can't be done?" I retorted. "It's just a matter of time."

Flora pondered, her mind a whirl of thoughts. "Perhaps, as we deliberate, Theo Thomas, with his gift of foresight, already knows—"

I interrupted with a laugh, "He knows I wouldn't waste time like this. He'd expect me to cut to the chase."

Flora conceded, her hand retreating. Her logic was sound; Theo would anticipate every move.

With renewed resolve, I yanked the lock free, the lid yielding to reveal another nested enigma—just as Harlan Brown had foretold. Each box, a replica of the last, shrank in size, a relentless Russian doll of secrets.

I hefted the smaller box with ease, repeating the ritual of force and unveiling yet another layer. Frustration mingled with amusement as I grumbled, "The old man had a peculiar sense of humor. No treasure warrants such a convoluted defense. Anyone could simply abscond with the entire collection."

Flora remained silent, her eyes reflecting the gravity of our task. Seven times I repeated the cycle, until the eighth box lay before us—not a box at all.

This final box stretched nearly 40 centimeters in length, its design mirroring the others with uncanny precision. The pièce de résistance was the chain lock, a nine-piece marvel of craftsmanship, each iteration smaller and more intricate. The eighth lock, diminutive and delicate, was a masterpiece in its own right. Its interlocking rings required deft handling, tweezers rather than fingers, to navigate the labyrinthine path to freedom.

Fashioned from the finest white copper, these locks were exquisite, objects of beauty and precision. The eighth lock gleamed, its intricacy magnified by its size. I hesitated, glancing at Flora, who urged me with urgency, "There's no time for delicacy now!"

I grinned, reluctant yet resolute. "I'd hate to damage such a work of art."

With a deft flick of my knife, the lock yielded, the buckle surrendering with a soft click. As the lid lifted, Flora and I gasped, our voices a harmonic "Ah!" that echoed through the room.

For all the anticipation, the box was a void, a hollow vessel devoid of content. Disbelief washed over me, my hand reaching into the emptiness as if to conjure something from nothing. It was a foolish gesture, and I withdrew, my cheeks flushed with embarrassment.

Frustration bubbled to the surface. "Is this some elaborate jest, old Theo's final prank from beyond? Why send me on this wild chase if there's nothing here?"

Flora, equally bewildered, finally found her voice. "Perhaps it's not about the contents."

"What do you mean?" I demanded.

Her response was a riddle in itself. "There are boxes."

I laughed, a dry, incredulous sound. "Boxes within boxes, and the last one empty. Is that supposed to be something?"

I gathered the boxes, one by one, returning them to their nest. The locks clattered into the larger box, the lid closing with a decisive thud. "Store it in the basement—a monument to futility."

Flora hesitated, a thoughtful look in her eyes. "What if we missed something? Perhaps there's a secret way to open it."

I scoffed. "An empty box is empty, no matter how you slice it."

She offered no retort, her silence a tacit understanding. I muttered, "Old Thomas had too much time on his hands, spinning tales and weaving nonsense."

Flora, ever perceptive, countered softly, "Yet you saw something, didn't you?"

Her words lingered in the air, a whisper of truth amidst the enigma. Theo Thomas's puzzle was more than a mere jest—it was a challenge, an invitation to seek beyond the obvious, to find meaning in the journey rather than the destination.

CHAPTER 6

RESPONSE FROM THE OBSERVATORY

I sat on the box, momentarily startled, and muttered, "Theo's words must have gotten to me. I must've had a hallucination."

Flora, ever composed, didn't challenge my claim. Instead, she prompted, "Describe this hallucination."

So I did. I recounted the vision that had played out before me. Flora listened intently, absorbing each detail. When I finished, she remarked, "It's uncanny. What you described aligns perfectly with the tales of old Theo."

"Exactly," I replied. "That's why I think it's just Theo's words playing tricks on my mind."

Flora's expression was thoughtful. "Neither Harlan Brown nor I saw it. But you did. Perhaps there's a celestial force influencing you."

I chuckled, adopting a theatrical tone. "Indeed, I must be a star descended from the heavens. You mere mortals should kneel and pay homage to your star god."

Flora gave me a mock glare and retreated upstairs.

I followed her, heading to the study where I unfurled a large star map across the desk.

Although I dismissed my vision as a "hallucination," the scene had etched itself into my memory. With the map before me, I pinpointed the seven stars that had radiated beams of starlight.

Most vivid in my recollection was the intersection of those beams—a bright red point nestled between the 8th and 13th stars of Virgo. It was the Pingdao star, one of the seven eastern stars, though no visible stars occupied that space between the two.

If I connected the eastern stars with imaginary lines, they formed a dragon. The convergence of the star rays was at the dragon's head, or more precisely, its mouth.

I closed my eyes, questioning the reality of my vision. The impression was so vivid. Had Theo Thomas seen this same celestial phenomenon? Was this the great disaster he alluded to, a cataclysm that had occurred only twice in history?

I pondered endlessly but found no answers.

As dawn approached, I left the study and returned to the bedroom. Before that, I had gazed at the night sky for what felt like an eternity, hoping for a repeat of the strange phenomenon. But the stars remained silent.

In the bedroom, Flora was already asleep. I lay beside her, tossing and turning, haunted by Theo Thomas's ominous warnings.

The following morning, I rose early, driven by the need to reach out to an acquaintance. We barely knew each other, having met once by chance. During our brief encounter, he had shared his thoughts on extraterrestrial life. He was an astronomer, working at the National Observatory of Belgium.

I recalled his words with clarity: "We will never fully grasp the secrets of the stars. Imagine trying to unravel the mysteries of celestial bodies from hundreds, thousands, even tens of thousands of light-years away. It's like observing a beautiful woman from a kilometer away and hoping to understand her essence."

His analogy had stuck with me. Humanity often boasts of its scientific achievements, believing that a century of progress has unveiled countless secrets of the universe. Yet, as I pondered the vastness of space, I realized how little we truly understood.

Many astronomers often tout the triumphs of their field, praising the capabilities of enormous telescopes and their potential to unravel the mysteries of the cosmos. Yet, how can we truly comprehend celestial bodies merely by observing them from afar? My friend's metaphor about this limitation was quite fitting.

This is why, when grappling with a complex astronomical issue, I find it prudent to consult a scholar who acknowledges the inherent limitations of human understanding of the universe. Such a scholar resides far away in Belgium, and it took me nearly half an hour to reach him by phone. Initially, the observatory staff informed me that Dr. Yinda was unavailable. However, when they realized the call was from the Far East, they asked me to try again later.

Belgium is seven hours behind my eastern city. It was eight in the morning here and just one in the morning there—the prime time for an astronomer to be immersed in the night sky.

I called back fifteen minutes later, and this time, someone answered. After a brief wait, a deep voice came on the line: "Who is this? Yinda speaking."

I quickly introduced myself. "This is Ash Morris. We met about three years ago. You once told me that observing stars through a telescope is like trying to understand a beautiful woman from a kilometer away."

The deep voice chuckled. "Yes, I remember. You mentioned that even marrying a beautiful woman doesn't guarantee understanding her."

I replied, "Exactly. You seemed quite disheartened then, saying that by my logic, astronomy doesn't truly exist, and even if we could reach a star, we still wouldn't comprehend it."

The voice sighed, "True enough. Humans have inhabited Earth for millennia, yet our understanding of it remains limited. How can we then claim to know other worlds?"

He paused, then asked, "So, how can I assist you, my friend?"

I hesitated, unsure how to explain. "It's rather peculiar. Last night, while star-gazing, I witnessed something quite unusual."

Yinda laughed. "Have you discovered a new star? That's the dream of every amateur astronomer. Share its location with me, and I'll verify it against our nightly astronomical records."

I quickly clarified, "No, not exactly. I'm curious about your knowledge of ancient Chinese astronomy."

There was a brief pause before Yinda replied with regret, "I'm afraid I know very little."

"That's alright," I said. "I saw something strange last night involving Virgo, Scorpio, Libra, and Sagittarius. Seven stars emitted fine beams of starlight eastward, converging between the 8th and 12th stars of Virgo, forming a bright red point for a fleeting moment. Everything transpired in an instant. I wonder if there's any record of this. From your perspective, what might explain such an occurrence?"

After a moment of silence, Yinda asked me to recount the experience. Once I did, he inquired, "What equipment were you using?"

"None," I admitted. "I observed it with my naked eye."

Dr. Yinda was silent again before saying, "I recall you mentioning that you often write fantasy fictions."

I couldn't help but chuckle, assuring him, "This isn't fiction. Another person witnessed it ten minutes before I did. What I'm trying to confirm is..."

I faltered, the surreal nature of the experience leaving me at a loss. What exactly was I hoping to confirm? That this celestial anomaly foretold a great disaster somewhere in the East? Dr. Yinda likely couldn't provide that answer.

What I truly needed to confirm was whether this phenomenon genuinely occurred, or if it was merely an illusion. After some thought, I said, "I want to know if what I saw was real. Specifically, have the stars in those constellations exhibited any abnormal behavior?"

Yinda responded, "I'll need to review the records, but I can tell you this: if the stars' activity was significant enough to be visible to the naked eye, it would mark a major celestial event. The observatory would receive reports from all over, and millions worldwide would have seen it."

I insisted, "Don't worry about it. Just check and let me know later."

Dr. Yinda agreed, and I added, "I'll call you back in an hour for the results."

With that, our first call ended. As I hung up the phone, I noticed Flora standing nearby.

I playfully exaggerated, "See? People love a bit of flattery. Now I feel like I've been chosen by destiny to save the world from disaster."

Flora laughed at my antics.

"If you really want to take action," she said, "you won't be following destiny's orders; you'll be defying them. If disaster is heaven's will, you'd be challenging it."

I raised my hands dramatically, "That's a tall order!"

Flora smiled, "I have some work to do in the basement. If it's urgent, you can find me there. Otherwise, please don't disturb me."

Though I was curious about her task, I respected her privacy. Instead, I joked, "No worries for now. But when I head to the stars, I hope you'll see me off."

With a smile, Flora headed downstairs.

I poured myself a glass of milk, then returned to the star map, pinpointing and noting the stars emitting those mysterious rays. As I wrote, the doorbell rang unexpectedly. I stood and heard Harlan Brown's voice, "Ash, something strange has happened."

I called out, "Come on up and tell me."

Harlan Brown bounded up the stairs, his excitement palpable despite the weariness etched on his face. His eyes were bloodshot, evidence of a sleepless night. Without preamble, he exclaimed, "Guess what I did after I got home last night?"

I cut to the chase, "Just tell me already."

Though momentarily taken aback by the rebuff, Harlan Brown's enthusiasm remained unflagging. He burst into the study, "I called around as soon as I got back. I reached out to 86 major observatories worldwide."

I raised an eyebrow, impressed, and gestured for him to sit. Harlan, flattered, sat briefly before springing up again, "I asked if they noticed any unusual activity in the stars old man Theo mentioned."

I nodded, appreciating his initiative. He had been more proactive than I, as I hadn't contacted Dr. Yinda until this morning.

Eager for his findings, I asked, "What did you find out?"

Harlan Brown pulled out a small notebook, his voice brimming with urgency. "Out of the 86 observatories I contacted, thirty-seven had nothing to report, forty-four observed no anomalies, but five of the largest ones recorded unusual spectrometer readings in Virgo, Scorpio, Sagittarius, and Libra. They couldn't pinpoint the cause, though."

I absorbed this information, my mind racing with possibilities. Harlan's voice rose in excitement. "Ash, those constellations correspond to the seven eastern stars in ancient Chinese astronomy. Old man Theo wasn't just speculating — the anomaly he predicted, with the Black Dragon and the seven stars aligning, really did happen."

I asked for the names of the five observatories, noticing that Dr. Yinda's wasn't among them. While most observatories provided general responses, the Belgian Observatory led by Dr. Yinda had simply replied "no comment" to Harlan Brown's inquiry. I waved my hand. "I also reached out to an astronomy expert. Let's wait for his insights."

Harlan Brown was insistent. "It's clear, Ash. The East is on the brink of a major catastrophe!"

His earnest concern was both infuriating and comical. He rubbed his hands together, a nervous gesture. "But I can't fathom what kind of disaster, nor where it will strike."

No one could answer those questions, of course. Harlan had a knack for posing the impossible. "Ash," he pressed, "Old Theo said you could avert the disaster. What will you do?"

I replied, exasperated, "Without knowing the disaster, how can I stop it? Let's not jump to conclusions."

Harlan reclined on the sofa, worry etched on his face. I sighed, "I apologize for not telling you everything yesterday— I was still processing it myself."

At this, Harlan's eyes widened with curiosity. I recounted the vision I had seen, and halfway through, he leapt up, visibly shaken. I illustrated the star map with starlights, using dashed lines to represent starlights, and pointed to the intersection. "What do you make of this point?"

Harlan pondered deeply, then gasped, "It's positioned right before the Black Dragon's mouth!"

I nodded. "Exactly. I noticed that last night. But what does it signify?"

Harlan scratched his head, lost in thought, muttering, "It's terrifying! The sky is warning us, yet we can't decipher it."

I sighed too. "If Theo Thomas were alive, he might have answers."

Harlan suddenly drew a deep breath, then said, "Perhaps he died because he uncovered a celestial secret."

He looked at me with a somber intensity, reminiscent of a warrior's farewell. I waved off the notion. "Don't cast me as a hero. I doubt a single person can avert such disaster. Theo might have heard something about me, thinking I could help."

Harlan was quick to encourage, "If you can intervene, then you must..."

I assured him, "I'll do my best, but for now, this phenomenon is merely compelling material for astrological study."

Harlan placed his hand on his forehead, recalling something important. "Theo Thomas mentioned this alignment happened twice before. I'll dig through the records to uncover what disasters those were."

I agreed with his plan. "Focus on Theo's collection. It's unparalleled in Chinese astronomy."

Harlan nodded, determined. "Yes! Though Mason Thomas is a tough nut to crack, I have my ways."

He patted his chest confidently, signaling his resolve to unearth the necessary information.

Time flew by as I spoke with Harlan Brown, and soon, it was nearly an hour since I had last spoken with Dr. Yinda. I gestured to Harlan to remain silent as I dialed the phone, putting the receiver on loudspeaker so he could hear the conversation as well.

The call connected, and Yinda's voice came through, sounding breathless and urgent. "Ash, you mentioned seeing seven stars with your naked eyes in Virgo... showing abnormal light?"

"Yes," I replied quickly. "What did your observatory's instruments record?"

Yinda took a moment, his voice still carrying an edge of disbelief. "You shouldn't be able to see it."

"Don't worry about that," I pressed. "Just tell me if there were any changes."

Harlan Brown tensed beside me as we both listened intently. Yinda continued, "Our latest spectrometer, linked to our computer system, indeed recorded spectral variations in seven stars. Those stars are in Virgo..."

As he listed the star names, Harlan marked them on our star map. Five matched the ones I'd marked earlier, though two differed slightly. I felt a sense of satisfaction;

recalling even approximate positions from memory was a significant feat, especially with five perfect matches.

Once Yinda finished, I asked, "And between Virgo and star number 12, what did you find?"

"The strangest thing," Yinda responded, "is that a seventh-magnitude star there suddenly increased in luminosity to third magnitude very briefly, as if it exploded. But then it returned to its original state, as if nothing happened."

"What does that mean?" I pressed.

Yinda sighed, "Who can say? Virgo is so distant from Earth. The scope of astronomical study is vast. I can assure you, though, that what our spectrometer recorded isn't visible to the naked eye. Absolutely sure."

I took a deep breath. "I won't dispute your certainty. Perhaps it's telepathic. An old man once told me that using the mind to sense celestial phenomena can be more insightful than observing them with eyes."

Yinda's voice was puzzled. "I don't understand..."

"That's astrology," I replied. "No need for you to understand that. But tell me, do changes in celestial bodies affect Earth?"

"Of course," he answered immediately. "The simplest example is how sunspot explosions can disrupt Earth's radio communications."

"So," I continued, "what impact might the changes in these seven stars, with a sudden brightening of seven stars, have on Earth?"

Yinda was silent for a while, then admitted, "You've stumped me. I doubt any astronomers have considered that. It's more an astrologer's domain."

I couldn't help but remark, "Ancient astrologers were astronomers who seemed to grasp more than modern ones."

Yinda protested, "That's not true!"

"You just acknowledged celestial changes can affect Earth, yet we don't know how. That's a gap in our scientific understanding," I pointed out.

"How do you know this?" Yinda asked, bewildered. "Globally, only our observatory and five others have equipment sensitive enough to detect this change."

"Yes, and those five observatories are far more forthcoming in public inquiries than yours," I remarked.

Yinda seemed momentarily puzzled by my comment, but I offered no explanation. Instead, I thanked him for his time and ended the call.

After hanging up the phone, a heavy silence settled between Harlan Brown and me, a silence thickened by the absurdity of our situation and the ominous weight of what we had just learned. The observatory's latest detection equipment had recorded a change—imperceptible to the naked eye, yet I had seen it as clearly as if it were etched in the sky.

Theo Thomas had seen it too. Not only had he seen it, but he understood its significance—a disaster of cosmic proportions. Could there be unseen celestial bodies, lurking in the vast tapestry of the universe, exerting their mysterious influence on him and me?

The concept felt surreal, alien. Could there be higher entities on these stars, their wisdom reaching across the void to touch Earth? Was it radiation from the stars themselves, or some other cosmic force altering our fate? Were we chosen by these celestial influences, or merely victims of cosmic chance? Could our altered behavior ripple through humanity, like stones cast into a pond?

These questions, swirling with no answers, seemed to tug at the very fabric of reality.

I sat there, watching Harlan Brown meticulously trace patterns on the star map, his voice a low murmur: "The seven stars in the east—imagine them as a dragon. The lines connect, forming the shape. What does the dragon symbolize?"

His words grated against my nerves. "Can you be quiet? Less talk, more thought."

Harlan Brown paused, then quietly asked, "Where is Flora? Her insights are always sharp."

I dismissed his question with a huff. Yet his musings lingered, taking root in my thoughts. "The dragon—could it represent a force? A powerful, consuming force. The star rays converge at its mouth, suggesting..."

He hesitated, the revelation hanging in the air. I picked up the thread, intrigued despite myself. "A powerful force poised to swallow something."

Harlan Brown's hand slapped the table, his eyes alight. "Yes! But how could it be a catastrophe?"

I countered, "Why not? A tsunami swallows all in its path—is that not a catastrophe?"

He met my gaze, solemn. "A tsunami's devastation is unstoppable."

"I never claimed to stop it. In China, the dragon symbolizes imperial power, a force from the highest echelons."

Harlan Brown nodded, thoughtful. "Interesting. What other emperors exist in the East? The Japanese emperor?"

His words struck a chord, a realization sparking between us. We spoke in unison, "The dragon—a potent symbol of Eastern power."

Harlan Brown leaned forward, urgency in his voice. "A powerful force, pointing... pointing..."

His words trailed into silence, leaving a void we couldn't fill. We sat, grappling with the enormity of it all, until I broke the stalemate. "Speculation is futile. Let's seek answers. We'll consult Mr. Thomas, search ancient texts for clues about the seven stars' alignment and the disasters foretold."

His relief was palpable, and together we descended the stairs, our path lit by the possibilities ahead. As we passed the basement door, I called out, "We're going to the Thomas family."

Flora's voice floated up, a simple acknowledgment, "Okay."

Arriving at the Thomas family estate, we found them ensconced in funeral preparations. Mason greeted us with a cold gaze. Had Harlan Brown come alone, he would have driven him away.

I explained our purpose, invoking the memory of his late brother. "This was Mr. Theo Thomas's final wish. He asked for my help. Would you deny him peace in his grave?"

The mention of his brother softened Mason's resolve, though reluctance lingered in his eyes. "Fine. You may read in brother's room, but do not wander."

We had what we came for. Stepping into the sanctum of Theo Thomas's room, we felt the weight of history and mystery pressing upon us, knowing that within these walls lay the threads of a puzzle that could alter our understanding of the universe itself.

CHAPTER 7

THE ANSWER TO THE EVIL SIGN

For the next seven days, we subsisted on our own provisions, while Harlan Brown and I immersed ourselves in Theo Thomas's sanctum, poring over a myriad of astronomical tomes. Serving as Theo Thomas's servant for a year had not been in vain for Harlan Brown; his grasp of ancient celestial lore far surpassed mine. The sheer volume of Theo Thomas's library was staggering—it would require a decade, if not more, to meticulously peruse every manuscript.

Harlan Brown's extensive knowledge proved invaluable. He could discern which texts were indispensable and which could be dismissed without a second glance. I entrusted this sifting task to him, dedicating myself instead to delving into Theo Thomas's meticulously kept records.

These records were a revelation. A staggering thirty bookcases brimmed with his meticulous observations of the heavens. His handwriting was a wild dance of cursive strokes, sometimes so minuscule that a magnifying glass was necessary, other times as bold as walnuts. It was clear he began chronicling the celestial ballet in his early twenties, continuing until his final breath — over seventy years of fervent dedication. His lexicon was archaic and obscure, a maze of words that left me reeling after seven days of relentless reading.

Yet, in this dizzying journey, I unearthed profound insights. Theo Thomas not only mastered the astrological wisdom of his forebears but also formulated unique interpretations. His predictions, once dismissed, now found validation.

Consider this entry: on the fourth day of the sixth month of Bingzi (1936), he noted, "The Tai Sui moved westward, stars flickered in the east, meteors streaked across the west of Tai Sui. This portends military strife from east to west. Could this foreshadow a great war for China?"

A mere year later, in the sixth month of Dingchou (1937), the Sino-Japanese War erupted. His prophecy rang true: "A year ago, Tai Sui's westward shift foretold military turmoil. Indeed, the great war was heralded by celestial signs.

Tai Sui emerged from the east, a harbinger of the Japanese forces advancing westward. Alas, had I foreseen this sooner."

His lament, "Alas, had I foreseen this sooner," struck me as a touch ironic. Even with foresight, what power did he wield to alter the heavens? "Tai Sui" is Jupiter, and its westward drift is a natural celestial motion observable from Earth. Even armed with prescience, could one defy Jupiter's celestial path?

Theo Thomas's foresight was not confined to war alone. He foresaw "great evils in the east," alluding to Japan's imperial aspirations. Yet, following the triumphant conclusion of the Sino-Japanese War, his records dwindled, save for one cryptic entry: "A shadow falls upon the Tian Star, a dire omen. A general shall meet a violent end." Three months hence, he appended a note: "Dai Li, plane crash." A startling prediction. For those unfamiliar, Dai Li was a renowned intelligence chief in modern Chinese history, perishing in an aviation accident near Nanjing. Theo Thomas divined this tragedy in the stars, yet its victim eluded him. The more I delved into his writings, the more I marveled at the scientific underpinnings and patterns governing celestial divination, and his extraordinary acuity was nothing short of astounding. However, after seven days,

Harlan Brown and I remained bereft of the elusive knowledge we sought.

For those seven intense days, Flora and I were like ships passing in the night, our paths rarely crossing. Her domain was the basement, a mysterious realm where she toiled away while I was ensnared in Theo Thomas's astronomical labyrinth.

One midnight, as I returned home weary from unraveling celestial secrets, I chanced upon her emerging from the depths below. Curiosity piqued, I couldn't help but ask, "What have you been up to down there?"

With a mischievous glint in her eye, she challenged me, "Push the door and see for yourself. Then you'll know."

I chuckled, "Do you really think I can't guess? If only I'd possessed my current grasp of astrology when I first met Theo Thomas, I might have understood his cryptic musings. No wonder he was disillusioned, thinking I was a mere pretender."

Flora laughed, a melody of confidence, "And yet, you still don't know what I'm doing."

I matched her laughter, "Oh, I'll figure it out eventually."Her smile turned cunning, "If you paid closer attention, you'd already know."

Her words stung, a gentle rebuke of my inattentiveness. I spread my hands in surrender, "Honestly, these last days have left me muddled, swimming in Theo Thomas's astronomical records."

I shared a few of Theo Thomas's entries with her, and she listened with keen interest, interjecting her thoughts. Yet, even as I spoke, my mind wandered back to the enigma of her basement activities. What could possibly require such prolonged dedication? My own focus had been consumed by the celestial dance, the myriad names of stars, both Eastern and Western, filling my thoughts.

Eventually, I conceded defeat, raising my hands in surrender, "Alright, I give up. I can't guess."

Flora's eyes twinkled as she said, "Alright, I'll give you a hint. What's missing in the house?"

I was taken aback. Surely, my attention wasn't so poor as to miss something obvious? I glanced around, scrutinizing our surroundings. Everything seemed in place. Reluctantly, I admitted, "Okay, give me another day. I'll figure it out."

She remained silent, confident in her challenge. Her hint suggested something significant was amiss, not a trivial item tucked away in a drawer. Yet, by the next morning, as Harlan Brown rang the bell summoning me back to Theo

Thomas's, the mystery remained unsolved. Flora had retreated once more to her clandestine work in the basement.

That day unfolded much like those before it, with Harlan Brown and I poring over records and tomes. Amid the sea of papers, I stumbled upon a crucial document, distinct in its texture and nestled amidst the chaotic stack. It beckoned with the mention of the Seven Eastern Mansions.

The note was ominous: "The Seven Eastern Mansions, led by the thirty Black Dragon stars , emit a crimson glow, heralding disaster just beginning. Clouds shroud the earth, calamity brews, and from this, the ruin of life commences. The light of these thirty stars clashes, and within two decades, they portend a bloody reckoning, suffering for the masses. How tragic!"

Beside the bold proclamations of doom, a subtle whisper in small script caught my eye: "The sky radiates dark and then brightens again, and there is another peaceful and prosperous era in the east, which is really an anomaly."

Theo Thomas's records were a tapestry of riddles, each requiring time and patience to unravel. These lines were no exception. They seemed to suggest that a sudden shift among the thirty main stars of the Seven Eastern Mansions heralded an impending catastrophe, a calamity so profound it threatened all life. Yet, intriguingly, there was a glimmer of hope—a paradoxical promise of a renewed era of peace in the east, where the celestial glow first dims before bursting into brilliance. A contradiction, indeed.

I mulled over the words, striving for clarity, before calling Harlan Brown over. "Take a look at these lines about the Seven Eastern Mansions. Do they carry any special significance?"

Harlan Brown, abandoning his book, turned to me, his brow furrowed with concentration. "It's not straightforward. The reference to the sky radiation... it lies within the Black Dragon's belly. What could it symbolize?"

"The coexistence of suffering and peace, this paradoxical notion, it's perplexing," I mused.

Harlan Brown flipped the note, revealing more scribbles on the reverse. "Look here, another note. It seems he calculated the influence of the thirty main stars of the Seven Eastern Mansions."

Eagerly, I examined the lines, deciphering the scrawled script alongside Harlan Brown. Though a few words eluded us, the essence of the passage became clear.

Theo Thomas's hurried handwriting revealed: "I spent a year calculating the motion of the thirty main stars of the Seven Mansions in the East. The result is a celestial secret, hidden in the most fitting place. It is ominous for those who discover it. In the future, when the seven stars have starlights, it will be revealed. Life and death will alternate, marking a new epoch."

Harlan Brown and I were struck silent, the weight of the revelation settling over us. I spoke first, breaking the oppressive silence: "This passage is clear: the thirty main stars influence the fates of thirty individuals. Theo Thomas even identified them, creating a concealed list. But now, as he foretold, the time of 'the seven stars having starlights' has arrived. The list should surface."

"Where could it be?" Harlan Brown asked, urgency in his voice.

"Patience," I advised. "We will find it if we search diligently."

Our newfound discovery fueled our determination, yet despite three days of meticulous searching, the elusive list remained hidden.

By the fourth day, the enigma of Flora's basement activities still eluded me. However, Harlan Brown stumbled upon another cryptic revelation buried within the pages of Theo Thomas's collection. It was akin to the mysterious "The Starlights of Seven Stars Linked Together" phenomenon but veiled in even deeper obscurity. The manuscript, handwritten and untitled, seemed almost mythical in its rarity. How Theo Thomas acquired it was a mystery in itself. The text revealed: "In the seventh month of the third year of Jianchu, the star lights of seven stars of the White Tiger were linked together and converged in the extreme west. It was a great ominous sign, ruling the extreme west. A year later, a large city was destroyed, and no one could escape."

Harlan Brown's voice was a blend of excitement and trepidation as he exclaimed, "Look at this! The convergence of the seven stars is a dire omen, foretelling the destruction of a large city."

I skimmed the text, my mind racing. "Indeed, this time it's the seven stars of the Western Stars aligning. A major city in the west was doomed. Jianchu... Jianchu... Under which emperor's reign was that?"

Harlan Brown sighed, rolling his eyes in exasperation. "With so many emperors in Chinese history, and reign titles so similar, who could possibly remember them all?"

His point was valid. Beyond the reigns of a few illustrious rulers, the myriad of reign titles blurred together in obscurity. Determined to pinpoint the timeline, I scoured our reference books. The name "Jianchu" resonated across three reigns: Emperor Zhang of the Eastern Han Dynasty, Yao Chang of the Later Qin Dynasty, and Li Song of the Western

Liang Dynasty, during the periods 76 to 84 AD, 386 to 394 AD, and 405 to 417 AD, respectively.

Translating the prophecy, the convergence of the seven stars supposedly occurred in "the seventh month of the third year of Jianchu," predicting disaster the following year. Thus, the catastrophic event must have transpired in one of these years: 79 AD, 389 AD, or 408 AD.

Harlan Brown and I laid out these years, scrutinizing their historical contexts. I pointed to "79 AD," suggesting, "79 AD seems too early. At that time, there might not have been any major western cities to destroy—"

My words trailed off as I caught Harlan Brown's gaze, his expression morphing into one of profound realization, a "click" sound escaping his throat.

His reaction was infectious. Realization dawned on me as well, and though I couldn't see my own face, I was certain that my expression mirrored his—wide-eyed and slack-jawed. An involuntary sound echoed from my throat as the pieces of the puzzle fell into place within my mind.

Harlan Brown and I both gasped, our exclamations of "Oh my God!" resonating in the charged air. The realization hit us like a tidal wave. We both recalled the catastrophe that befell the West in 79 AD—a tragedy etched into the annals of human history. The Roman Empire, then at its zenith, had counted Pompeii among its most vibrant cities. In August of that year, Mount Vesuvius erupted, burying the city in a suffocating shroud of lava and ash, annihilating its populace without mercy.

August of 79 AD corresponded with July of the sixth year of Jianchu in the reign of Emperor Zhang of the Eastern Han Dynasty. The celestial convergence of the seven western stars had indeed heralded the city's doom.

The linkage of the seven stars was an omen of great consequence, foretelling the obliteration of a major city.

Now, the ominous alignment of the seven eastern stars loomed large, suggesting a similar fate awaited a great city in the East. This destruction was prophesied to occur the year following the celestial event.

In 79 AD, the loss of life in Pompeii was immeasurable, but even then, a city's population would scarcely reach 100,000. In contrast, today's metropolises boast millions. The thought of such a city facing complete destruction was beyond comprehension.

Theo Thomas's desperate cries of "living things are in ruins" made perfect sense in this context. His attempts to avert the impending disaster were fevered, ultimately consuming him.

As I pondered this revelation, a tumult of thoughts swirled within me, leaving me with a singular sensation: sheer shock and dread.

I had been a skeptic, dismissive of the notion that celestial bodies could exert influence over earthly affairs. Yet, Theo Thomas's records had swayed my beliefs. The interplay of stars and their vast cosmic forces seemed capable of influencing earthly "actions," from the rhythmic tides and the transmission of radio waves to the behaviors and emotions of living beings. Psychologists have long acknowledged the moon's effect on human psychology and emotions. The moon, though close, is but a minor star in the cosmic expanse. Yet, its influence is undeniable.

Harlan Brown, visibly shaken, stood speechless. His mouth agape, perspiration glistening on his brow. After a prolonged silence, I managed to articulate my thoughts: "I've realized it — the linkage of the seven stars signals the destruction of a major city."

Harlan Brown, his voice a strangled croak, asked, "Which city is it?"

The question loomed large. The East was home to many grand cities. Which one would bear this ominous fate? Before I could respond, Harlan Brown's voice cut through the air, sharp and decisive: "Tokyo! I believe it's Tokyo in Japan."

I inhaled sharply, the pieces clicking into place. "The Great Kanto Earthquake of 1923 — geologists have long posited that such catastrophic quakes recur every 60 years, each surpassing the last in magnitude. So, next year... Could it be that Tokyo faces obliteration in the impending earthquake?"

Harlan Brown murmured, his voice barely above a whisper, "No one is spared, no one is spared... How many souls call Tokyo home now?"

I couldn't help but smile wryly at the situation. "During the day, Tokyo swells with more than 10 million people, though about 60% remain at night. This earthquake... it's said to strike within a year."

Harlan Brown wiped his brow, his expression shifting to one of perplexity. "What ties did Theo Thomas have with Japan? Why did he implore you so fervently to save the Japanese?"

His comment tugged a bittersweet smile from me. I waved my hands dismissively. "You give me too much credit. Even if we pinpoint Tokyo's destruction by an earthquake in a year, what could I possibly do to avert it?"

Harlan Brown nodded, acknowledging the truth. "Indeed, even with your capabilities, the task seems insurmountable. Were you to go to Japan, announce this at a press conference, urging an exodus from Tokyo—"

"Enough!" I interrupted, my voice firm. "If we did that, we'd only end up in a mental institution."

Harlan Brown sighed, resigned. "True, no one would heed such a warning. Just as in our city, if two strangers declared its impending doom within a year, the populace would dismiss it as madness."

"Precisely," I agreed. "So, even armed with this knowledge, our hands are tied."

Harlan Brown's attempt at levity was almost comical. "At least we could warn our acquaintances to avoid Tokyo next year."

I chuckled, waving him off. "That's a start, I suppose."

Silence enveloped us as we stared at Theo Thomas's empty bed, the echoes of his final days replaying in my mind. Memories of that stormy night, his urgent whispers, now clearer, yet still shrouded in mystery.

Theo Thomas's frantic cries to "stop them" echoed in my thoughts. What was I meant to stop? The stars themselves? The powers threatening a city? His warnings were prophetic, yet cryptic.

As I pondered, Harlan Brown broke the silence. "Ash, hold on a moment."

I looked up, intrigued. He took a breath before speaking. "Perhaps it's not an earthquake in Tokyo."

"What else could it be?" I asked, curious.

"Theo Thomas urged you to 'stop them,' remember? If the disaster were an earthquake, you couldn't prevent it."

I nodded, conceding his point. "True, no force can halt a natural catastrophe poised to destroy a city."

Harlan Brown hesitated, then posed a thought-provoking question. "What forces could obliterate a city, making escape impossible?"

He listed earthquakes, volcanic eruptions, tsunamis—all natural phenomena beyond human control.

I added, "These are all geological upheavals, colossal in their impact."

Harlan Brown continued, "And what about a massive cyclone?"

I shook my head. "A cyclone can ravage parts, but not obliterate an entire city."

Then he mentioned, "Nuclear weapons attack."

The thought struck me, cold and terrifying. A nuclear assault, especially one of significant scale...

Such an event would surpass the destruction of a single city. Was the threat a nuclear accident?

"It's possible," I mused aloud. "These forces align with the prophecy."

Harlan Brown reflected, "Natural disasters defy human intervention. Only human actions are preventable. So, could it be a nuclear conflict?"

I remained silent, grappling with the implications. Even against the specter of nuclear war, how could I intervene? A barrage of nuclear missiles would spell doom for any target.

Harlan Brown sighed, defeated. "I can't fathom any other scenarios. What do you think?"

I shrugged, acceptance settling in. "We've gleaned what we could. We needn't return."

Harlan Brown lingered, reluctant. "So many books here. I could spend years exploring them."

I gestured for him to join me, and we descended the stairs. There, we encountered Mason Thomas. The brothers had shared a close bond, and though Mason Thomas ignored astrology, his brother might have confided in him.

Approaching him, I asked, "Mr. Thomas, could we talk?"

Mason Thomas hesitated, then agreed. Harlan Brown called out, and I suggested returning to his brother's room.

Mason Thomas's gaze swept the room, a sadness in his eyes. He asked, "Did you open the box to see what was inside?"

Disappointment tinged my response. "I did, but there was nothing..."

Then, a revelation struck me, sudden and clear. I understood what Flora had been up to all these days.

CHAPTER 8

A NEW THEORY OF LIFE

Mason Thomas's mention of the black lacquer and gold-painted box sparked a realization about Flora's recent activities. She had been engrossed in unlocking those intricate nine-piece chain locks in the basement! Flora had always been inclined toward unique ideas. While I had opted for the brute-force method, dismantling the locks to reveal nested boxes, Flora believed there was a deeper purpose behind Theo Thomas's complex locking system.

She had insisted on patiently unlocking them, convinced that the method of opening might alter the outcome. This seemed odd to me—an empty box is empty regardless of how you open it. Yet, Flora had reassembled the locks, intent on exploring whether a different approach might yield different results. She had hinted earlier that something was missing, referring to the box itself, which I had dismissed as unimportant, given its emptiness.

Now, understanding her determination, I wondered how far she had progressed with those locks. The complexity of the nine-piece chain lock, especially the smallest one, was daunting, requiring precise tools and considerable effort.

I resolved to confront her upon my return, to share my insight and persuade her to abandon the task.

Meanwhile, Mason Thomas was visibly puzzled by my account. "Nothing in the box?" he echoed, incredulous.

I spread my hands in confirmation. "Yes, empty. A series of nested boxes, each with a nine-piece chain lock, leading to an empty core."

Mason Thomas's expression turned thoughtful. "Truly, my brother's actions were enigmatic."

Harlan Brown interjected skeptically. "I can't believe you bypassed the locks so swiftly."

I grinned, miming the action of forcibly removing the locks. "The box was mine, and I lacked the patience for delicate unlocking."

Harlan Brown shook his head, disapproving. "Ash, you've missed the point. Mr. Theo Thomas must have had a reason."

I chuckled. "Perhaps, but I suspect the true purpose was to entice curious minds like yours into a time-consuming puzzle."

Harlan Brown appeared disgruntled, but Mason Thomas seemed to dismiss the matter, settling into a chair as I summarized our findings. He listened with a mix of impatience and amusement.

When I finished, he chuckled. "Mr.Morris, my brother seems to have overestimated your abilities to avert disaster."

I spread my hands again, conceding the truth. "Indeed. Our goal was to glean more information. Some of Mr. Theo's last words seemed cryptic, yet potentially crucial."

Mason Thomas shook his head, resigned. "I'm afraid I can't assist you there. I couldn't decipher his words, much less retain them."

I pressed on. "But you once mentioned he wanted to meet me. Surely he had a reason. Do you recall that conversation?"

Mason Thomas frowned, sifting through memories. "The first time he mentioned you was when Finley Evans visited. He summoned me during their conversation···"

Mason Thomas recounted the scene: Theo Thomas, reclining in bed, Finley Evans at his side. Upon Mason's arrival, Theo instructed, "Find a man named Ash Morris and bring him to me."

Accustomed to his brother's eccentricity, Mason Thomas agreed, knowing his brother might forget by the next day. Yet, he lingered, overhearing Theo Thomas's ominous words: "The starlights of the eastern stars have appeared, foretold to align and heralding impending disaster!"

Finley Evans had sighed, "Heaven is unyielding. What can we do?"

Theo Thomas replied, "If we entrust the right person, hope remains."

Finley Evans had concurred, "Yes, Mr. Morris is extraordinary. Let him be our savior."

* * *

Mason Thomas paused, glancing at me. "I left after that."

Harlan Brown leapt to his feet, pointing at me. "Did you hear that? Despite the impending disaster, they foresaw a savior—perhaps you!"

I smiled ruefully, gesturing to my head. "Do you see any divine auras above me?"

Harlan Brown, chastened, fell silent. I turned back to Mason Thomas. "Did he mention me again?"

Mason Thomas nodded. "He forgot the next day, and I had no means to find you. But as his health declined, he grew more insistent. When I heard your name, I seized the chance to contact you."

My heart sank, the trail growing cold. I persisted. "And after Finley Evans's passing?"

Mason Thomas sighed, recalling. "On the day of Finley Evans's funeral, he insisted on attending, despite his frailty. I accompanied him, staying by Finley's side for a long time. Finley Evans was his only friend, and his grief was palpable."

I prompted, "Did he say anything to Mr. Evans's body?"

Mason Thomas paused, reflecting on that poignant moment.

Mason Thomas nodded gravely. "Yes, he lingered for a long time, then called out Finley Evans 's name and said, 'You left before me. Now I alone know that a great disaster is coming. Whoever, apart from me, sees the strange phenomenon of seven stars aligning will be the lucky star.' Just those sentences."

Despite his calm delivery, I was taken aback. Harlan Brown pointed to my forehead and exclaimed, "Did you hear that? You are a lucky star, a lucky star that fights against evil signs."

At that moment, an overwhelming fatigue washed over me. The enormity of the task before me—so vague and unpredictable—was exhausting.

I rubbed my face hard. "I just envisioned another possible destruction of an entire city."

Harlan Brown's eyes widened in shock. I continued, "If an asteroid were to suddenly veer off its trajectory and head towards Earth, even one just a kilometer in diameter could obliterate a large city."

Harlan Brown stammered, "Even a smaller one could cause significant devastation."

I spread my hands in exasperation. "What do you expect me to do? Like Superman, flying into the sky to catch the asteroid and redirect it?"

Harlan Brown had no immediate response, but he was persistent, muttering, "In short... you are a lucky star... only if you witness the strange phenomenon of the seven stars in the Eastern Seven Mansions. Maybe... that represents another form of destructive power you can stop."

Though weariness seeped into my voice, I spoke with unwavering resolve. "From now on, I choose to forget this matter and treat it as a nightmare."

Harlan Brown stared at me in disbelief as I turned to bid farewell to Mason Thomas. He chased after me, "If I figure out that destructive power..."

I sighed. "Don't waste your thoughts. As I've said before, if a force can destroy a city, it can't be stopped by one person alone."

Harlan Brown persisted. "Who said it must be your power alone? You might mobilize others to combat the destructive force."

I took a slow, deep breath. Harlan Brown's words were not entirely unreasonable. "Alright," I conceded. "Let's try to find out what kind of destructive power it is." I conceded, patting his shoulder. "Perhaps you're the true lucky star here."

Harlan Brown, with a solemn demeanor, said, "That's nothing strange. Many people on Earth are affected by billions of stars. I believe there is a special ability within the human brain. Each person possesses different capabilities. The billions of varied rays emitted by countless stars are filled with diverse energies. These energies can interact with an individual's brain activity, influencing their talents, thoughts, actions, and even personality."

We had just exited the Thomas family's mansion when I heard him continue. His systematic speech left me in awe, and I found myself nodding in agreement. "Your perspective is refreshing. The idea that different people have varying personalities and talents is both mysterious and incredible. Modern science cannot fully explain where genius originates or what determines personality. Your hypothesis that people are influenced by the radiative energy of different stars is truly groundbreaking."

Harlan Brown's excitement was palpable, his voice rising. "Think about it—Mozart could compose music at the age of four, Edison invented hundreds of devices in his lifetime, and Einstein's theory of relativity remains at the forefront of science. Some are born politicians, some scientists, some mediocrities, and some brilliant minds. These differences result from the influence of various stars."

I patted him on the back. "If two people have similar personalities and talents, it might be because the same star influences them."

Harlan Brown agreed. "Exactly. This is what I have learned from my research over the past year. I believe that a person is influenced by stars from the moment they leave the womb. The movement of the universe and stars plays a decisive role as they come into the world."

I added thoughtfully, "Your theory also explains why divination can predict a person's fate based on their precise birth time."

Harlan Brown's enthusiasm grew. "There are many facts to support my theory. Westerners divide birth months and days into twelve constellations. They've long observed that doctors, artists, and others often belong to the same constellations."

It was afternoon then, and I couldn't see a single star in the sky. Even at night, the stars visible to the naked eye are probably only a billionth of those in the universe.

The number of stars far exceeds the number of people on Earth, and everyone might be influenced by more than one star at times.

Harlan Brown seemed to read my thoughts. "Of course, not everyone is fortunate enough to be influenced by stars. But why are standout figures in African tribes, such as wizards, chiefs, hunters, and warriors, so exceptional? There is some mysterious power that endows them with talents."

As we approached the car, I gestured for Harlan Brown to get in first.

Harlan Brown got into the car, his excitement remain. "In the past, there were many mysteries I couldn't unravel, such as human destiny, which is extremely enigmatic. Take China, for example. During wartime, farmers from the same village enlisted together. Why did some perish in battle, others remain mere soldiers, while a few rose to become generals and marshals after ten or eight years? Destiny is influenced by the stars."

I looked at him. "You've devised a novel argument, undoubtedly influenced by a particular star."

I said this without a hint of mockery, and Harlan Brown didn't diminish his own contribution. "Of course, all human endeavors stem from this. But I don't know which star it is—perhaps it's millions of light years away from Earth."

This "mysterious radiation power of stars affecting human brain activity" theory couldn't be proven with concrete evidence, but as Harlan Brown articulated, it could explain the origins of human destiny, talent, temperament, and actions.

I drove Harlan Brown home, and he reminded me, "Don't forget that you are the lucky star to counter the evil signs of the Seven Stars Alliance this time."

I reluctantly agreed and headed straight home. As soon as I entered, I made a beeline for the basement door and knocked vigorously. "You don't have to waste time on those locks."

I called out twice but heard no response from Flora. Assuming she wasn't in the basement, I pushed the door, but it was locked. I called out again, and then I heard a "click." The door opened from the inside—it was Flora.

Immediately, I noticed several black lacquered gold boxes in the middle of the basement. There were nine boxes in total, all with their lids open. It seemed Flora had accomplished her "feat." Even the nine-piece chain lock on the smallest box had been opened correctly.

On a table, there were white copper rings of various sizes, clearly taken off the locks. Each nine-piece chain had 18 copper rings, totaling 144 in the eight locks. The largest had a diameter of 5 cm, while the smallest was less than one-tenth that size. I shook my head, "Great! Did you find anything?"

Only then did I notice Flora's pallid face. She leaned against the table, barely able to stand. It was evident she was extremely shaken. Alarmed, I quickly scanned the room to determine what had caused Flora's shocking reaction. To evoke such an expression, it had to be something serious.

Alarmed, I scanned the room for any sign of danger, but found nothing out of the ordinary. What had she discovered that warranted such a reaction?

My heart raced with curiosity and concern as I asked, "Did you really find anything in the box?"

It seemed impossible. I had opened every box, large and small, and there was nothing inside. An empty box, regardless of how it's opened, remains an empty box. I was convinced of this.

Despite my skepticism, Flora's reaction hinted at something unexpected. She had calmed down somewhat, but her voice still carried a trace of unease. "No, I didn't find anything in the box," she replied.

I approached her, holding her hand, and noticed it was cold to the touch, which heightened my alarm. I gently embraced her, repeating, "What happened, what happened?"

She rested her head on my shoulder, her breathing gradually steadying. After a moment, she pulled back, brushing her hair away from her face, her expression now composed. Seeing my worry, she offered a reassuring smile. "Don't worry," she said softly.

"But your hands are still cold," I insisted. "Something happened, didn't it?"

Flora lowered her gaze, admitting, "I've made some discoveries, but I'm not sure what they mean yet. Please, don't press me for details. I'll share everything once I have more clarity, okay?"

Her words were both frustrating and intriguing. She knew my impatience with mysteries, yet she was resolute in withholding information until she was ready. I realized that pushing her further would be futile.

"Could you at least give me a hint?" I pleaded.

She sighed. "I wish I could, but even I don't fully understand what I've found."

I scanned the basement again, noting the open boxes but nothing else out of the ordinary. There was no visible clue as to what had unsettled her so much.It was clear that whatever Flora had discovered had shaken her deeply, and it likely stemmed from the contents — or lack thereof — in those boxes. Her discovery had to be something profound, occurring just before my arrival.

I cast another glance at the array of boxes, and Flora discouraged my scrutiny. "Don't waste your time on those boxes," she advised.

Trying to lighten the mood, I teased, "Are you hiding a mistake you made?"

She sighed again, a mix of frustration and amusement. "Think what you will. You just don't understand..."

Abruptly shifting gears, she asked, "Why are you back so early today? Did you make a discovery?"

Seizing the opportunity, I replied, "Yes, a significant one. How about we trade discoveries?"

I settled myself comfortably on the cushions beside Flora, recounting our findings. "Harlan Brown and I discovered records indicating that the alignment of seven stars in 78 AD foreshadowed the destruction of a major city a year later."

Flora immediately connected the dots. "Pompeii!" she exclaimed.

"Exactly," I confirmed. "This time, the seven stars in the east might be a similar omen..."

"...for the destruction of a major city in the east," Flora finished my thought, her voice tinged with concern.

I adjusted my posture, more relaxed now, and recounted what Mason had told us, my discussions with Harlan Brown, and his intriguing theories. "I fear Old Theo might have misinterpreted this time. The forces capable of obliterating a city are beyond human control."

Flora pondered silently, then spoke thoughtfully. "You've considered numerous destructive forces — earthquakes, tsunamis, even rogue asteroids."

"Yes, we've explored various scenarios capable of devastating a metropolis..." I began, but Flora gestured for silence, deep in contemplation. I watched her, curious, as she remained lost in thought.

"What is it?" I prompted gently.

Flora appeared perplexed. "It's still just a nebulous idea. Harlan Brown's theory is fascinating—each person being influenced by their own unique star."

Her sudden shift in topic caught me off guard, but I responded nonetheless. "That idea resonates. Those touched by their stars to achieve greatness must indeed have prominent celestial influences."

I recalled a note from Theo Thomas's records. "Theo shared a similar belief, though in astrological terms rather than modern language."

Flora's curiosity was piqued. "What exactly did he say?"

I reflected on the records. "He noted that the eastern host stars numbered thirty, each representing a person. He even identified those thirty individuals by name. He warned of chaos, suffering, and bloodshed, all originating from these influences."

Flora processed this revelation slowly. "Could it mean that these thirty stars are impacting thirty individuals on Earth, driving them to extraordinary actions?"

"That seems to be his theory," I agreed. "He speculated that during Huang Chao's rebellion, which claimed millions of lives, the stars would have shown clear signs. He also predicted these thirty figures would clash within two decades..."

I trailed off, as the implications began to crystallize in my mind. The celestial phenomena observed by Theo Thomas—the transition of the Tianradi Star from dim to bright—seemed to symbolize the duality of calamity and prosperity. In light of current global tensions, I was momentarily overwhelmed, unable to articulate my thoughts.

Flora watched me, concerned. "What is it?" she asked gently.

I took a deep breath and shared my realization. "Theo Thomas had already received insights from the stars about the changes of the past thirty years."

Flora, looking slightly pensive, nodded in agreement. "Yes, the stars have been offering warnings for a long time."

We fell into silence, grappling with the magnitude of what we had uncovered. The symbols and omens seemed so stark, it was unsettling.

After some time, I continued, "Harlan Brown and I initially thought the destruction of a major city in the East might mean a catastrophic earthquake in Tokyo."

Flora gave a faint, resigned smile. "Quite a reasonable thought. But there's nothing we can do now. Perhaps it's best to forget these things."

Originally, this mirrored my own thoughts — I had advised Harlan Brown to treat it all as a nightmare. Yet, Flora's demeanor suggested she had discovered something significant, and her reluctance to share it made me hesitant to let the matter rest.

Determined, I said, "I won't give up until you tell me what you found. Remember, I'm supposed to be the 'lucky star' in this scenario."

Flora chuckled. "I've told you, it's just a vague idea. If I had anything concrete, I'd share it with you."

She then stood abruptly, pacing the room before fiddling with the copper rings on the table. It was clear she was lost in thought.

I gave her space as she toyed with the rings. Eventually, she seemed to reach a decision. Turning to me, she waved a dismissive hand. "I've decided to forget about the whole thing. If the disaster is inevitable, then nothing can stop it. Your 'lucky star' status won't change a thing."

I nodded, resigned. "For now, that seems like the only option."

That night, we sought distraction. After dinner, we went to a gathering at a friend's house. The atmosphere was lively, with many people in attendance. I even called Harlan Brown to join us. Amidst drinks and conversation, I posed a question to the group: "Can anyone propose a force capable of destroying a major city?"

The responses were varied but predictable — earthquakes, plagues, nuclear wars — the very scenarios Harlan Brown and I had contemplated.

But one individual's answer stood out. He suggested, "A big city is a hub for people because of what it offers. If suddenly, everyone decided to leave, the city would be effectively destroyed."

It was a novel perspective. He elaborated, "During the gold rush in the western United States, towns sprang up overnight. Once the gold was gone, so were the people, leaving ghost towns behind."

I countered, "But those were small towns. We're talking about cities with populations in the millions."

The friend laughed, conceding, "True, but even earthquakes and nuclear wars don't completely erase a city. Something always survives."

Harlan Brown interjected, "Mount Vesuvius's eruption annihilated Pompeii."

The friend nodded. "Pompeii was a major city for its time, but compared to today's metropolises, it was small."

Harlan Brown was momentarily stumped. The conversation shifted, and soon he was discussing his astrological research.

As expected, people were eager to hear about their destinies, and Harlan Brown became the center of attention, explaining his theory about cosmic influences on human fate.

The discussion was animated and engaging. Sensing the mood, I caught Flora's eye, nodded our goodbyes to the host, and we quietly slipped away into the night.

The night was peaceful, a perfect backdrop as we drove to a secluded spot and leaned against the car, gazing at the vast expanse of stars above. The familiarity with the stars I'd gained recently made the night feel even more profound. It was humbling to think about how, throughout history, only a select few have discerned the significant impacts these celestial bodies could have on Earth.

As we watched, a thought struck me. "Remember when we first met Theo Thomas and discussed astrology? You disagreed with the idea that the mysterious influence comes from advanced beings on planets. I argued it couldn't just come from a stone, and you said I had a point. What did you mean?"

Flora gestured to the sky. "It's simple. Every star up there is essentially a stone, just a much larger one."

Her explanation made me chuckle. "I see what you mean."

"But consider this," Flora continued. "With so many of these celestial stones, combined with the vastness of space, the universe becomes an endless arena of forces that could influence life on Earth. Even with millennia of study, humanity might never fully comprehend it."

I pondered her words, then asked, "So, do you agree with Harlan Brown's theory?"

Flora paused, deliberating before nodding slowly, indicating a degree of uncertainty. "The influence from stars is likely ever-changing," she mused. "If this influence shifts, then theoretically, the thoughts and behaviors of the person it affects would also change. Does that make sense?"

Her hypothesis was complex, almost abstract, and it took me a moment to process. "Let's hypothesize that this mysterious influence is a form of radiation energy," I suggested. "If it interacts with human brains, altering thoughts and actions, then a change in this energy could mean a person becomes unaffected by a particular star."

"Exactly," Flora agreed. "Which means that person has fundamentally changed."

I gave a wry smile at the theoretical nature of our discussion. "Yes, in theory."

Yet, Flora seemed deeply absorbed by the stars, contemplating our conversation's implications. After a long silence, she sighed, "Let's head back."

I secretly hoped to catch another glimpse of the unique alignment of the Black Dragon's seven stars, but such phenomena are rare, often visible only under specific conditions. I'd strained my neck looking for something that wasn't there.

Back home, Flora acted as though nothing had transpired. She avoided any mention of astrology, and I followed suit. When morning came, she was already out. Driven by curiosity, I spent half the day meticulously examining the nine boxes in the basement, searching for something—anything—that might explain her earlier reaction.

The process of opening the nine nine-piece chain locks had been arduous, taking Flora over ten days to complete. Yet, the boxes were undeniably empty, devoid of hidden compartments or secrets.

Frustrated, I decided to leave the basement. As I turned to go, I accidentally bumped into the table, causing the copper rings to jingle and clatter. My mind was a whirlwind of thoughts, and I absentmindedly picked up one of the rings to fiddle with it, all the while staring at the empty boxes. It was then that I noticed something peculiar—the ring in my hand had changed shape.

Upon closer inspection, I saw that the copper ring had hinges that allowed it to straighten into four arcs. This discovery piqued my curiosity, and I began examining the other rings. Each ring, regardless of size, shared this feature.

As I pulled apart a dozen or so rings, I discovered intricate engravings on them. At first glance, these engravings seemed random and lacked any discernible pattern. However, when I placed two rings of the same size side by side, something clicked.

The arcs from the rings, once aligned, could be placed next to each other. I arranged the 18 largest rings, noticing that the engravings connected to form a cohesive image. I stepped back, astonished by the sight before me.

It was a map—a map that would be recognizable to almost anyone. Scattered across this map were black dots, varying in size.

Initially, these dots seemed like imperfections in the white copper—ordinary flaws that didn't warrant attention. But with the rings arranged into a map, their significance became apparent. These dots were markers.

Conventionally, dots on a map denote locations; larger dots signify larger places, and smaller ones, smaller locations. However, upon closer examination, the black dots on this map didn't align with known cities or locations. Near the map's center, six black dots clustered together, with one notably larger than the others. This density of dots didn't correspond to any known urban area.

Additionally, another large black dot appeared in a place where no city should exist.

Puzzled, I wondered what these black dots could represent. If not cities, then what? They seemed to signify something significant, but without a clear understanding, their meaning remained elusive. It was a mystery that begged for further exploration.

CHAPTER 9

SECRETS IN EMPTY BOXES

Staring at the map formed by the copper rings, I wrestled with the question of what the black dots represented. It couldn't be a product distribution map, as the dense cluster of dots in the center didn't correspond to any known resource. Population density was also ruled out; the familiar shape of the map made it clear the dots didn't match the expected population centers.

I methodically arranged all the copper rings by size, noting that each formed a similar map with varying numbers of black dots. The largest ring had thirty dots, while the smallest had only seven. Intriguingly, one large dot in the southwest appeared consistently across all the maps.

The decreasing number of dots suggested a progression, but the meaning eluded me. Despite my skills in decoding and deciphering secrets, I couldn't crack this puzzle. Frustrated, I moved away from the table, sitting down to clear my mind with a cigarette. As I pondered, Flora's earlier demeanor and our conversation replayed in my mind. A sudden realization hit me, and I called out, "Flora!"

Her response was immediate, startling me. "I'm here, no need to shout," she replied.

I turned to see her standing at the basement door. She must have been watching for some time, unnoticed while I was absorbed in thought.

Flora met my gaze with a knowing look. I gestured for her to join me at the table, pointing to the copper rings. "Look at these black spots. You'll never guess what they mean."

With a serene smile, Flora replied, "Surprising? I've guessed, and I know you have too."

We exchanged a glance, and I suggested we say it together. In unison, we both said, "People."

The word hung in the air, and a profound silence enveloped the room. The realization that the black dots represented people brought a chilling clarity.

I knocked my head in frustration, prompting Flora to ask, "Did you figure something out?"

I shook my head slowly, my expression uncertain. "It's just a vague idea, nothing concrete yet..."

Her words mirrored my own earlier thoughts, highlighting that we were both contemplating the same puzzle. Flora had already deduced the significance of the black dots on the copper rings by the time I returned.

Recognizing our shared understanding made it easier to discuss the implications. I pointed to the copper rings. "These are the culmination of Theo Thomas's decades of celestial observations. The thirty black dots represent thirty individuals, each influenced by one of the thirty primary stars in the Eastern Seven Mansions. Their thoughts and actions can be anticipated by observing changes in these stars."

Flora nodded. "Yes, we talked about this—the idea that altering the stars, even slightly, would change those individuals' thoughts and actions."

I considered this, nodding slowly. It was a mind-bending concept. First, that human behavior could be influenced by celestial bodies; second, that changing celestial conditions was beyond human capability.

"Indeed," I continued. "Hypothetically, if we could decrease the brightness of Fang Star Four, it might alter the intelligence, courage, or even the aggression of the person influenced by it."

Flora gestured slowly to the copper rings on the table. Our thoughts were so abstract and speculative that they seemed almost surreal. "Theo Thomas cleverly used people's birthplaces to represent them," she noted.

"And the size of the black dots indicates their significance," I added.

Flora pointed to the largest dot in the center of the map on the first copper ring. It was surrounded by a cluster of dots, varying in size, but the largest dot stood out prominently. As she began to speak, I stopped her. "Don't say it."

She looked at me, puzzled. "Why not?"

I gave a wry smile. "We all know who it represents. There's no need to say it out loud."

Flora sighed, understandingly, and let it go. She then pointed to the smallest copper ring, which had seven black dots. Again, she indicated the largest dot, and we exchanged a knowing look. We both understood its significance.

In a hushed voice, Flora observed, "The black dots decrease progressively, indicating these individuals are gradually disappearing."

"Indeed," I agreed. "There are eight sets of copper rings, each with fewer dots. The earlier sets differ by just one or two dots, but the gaps widen in the later sets."

Flora added, "Yes, the older these people are, the more likely they are to die."

I considered her words. "What do you think? Does each set of rings represent a fixed time span, like five or four years?"

Flora examined the intricate engravings on the rings, thinking it over. "I don't believe so. I think they signify different periods. It could be ten years, or just one. Each represents a period marked by a significant event."

I immediately resonated with Flora's perspective. "Yes, look at this group, and the next one—there are nine fewer black spots. That period must be..." I hesitated for a moment, letting the weight of the realization sink in.

Flora continued in a slow, deliberate tone, "That period is ten years. It's evident what transpired in those ten years."

We both fell silent, contemplating the implications. Finally, I sighed, "Each group of copper rings represents a brutal war. Some fell during these conflicts, and the black spots representing them vanished in the next set of rings. These wars varied in scale, sometimes notorious, sometimes shrouded in secrecy. But they were invariably cruel, employing every conceivable human means, with a level of carnage beyond imagination."

Flora sighed as well, "Indeed, these individuals, influenced by celestial forces, possess talents far beyond the ordinary. Originally, no earthly power could easily destroy them. Their only true threat comes from their own infighting."

I pondered her words, murmuring, "Perhaps, even their mutual destruction is a cosmic influence."

Flora added, "Certainly, history is rife with such examples. Many powerful figures, known for their exceptional abilities, often dealt ruthlessly with those closest to them, even violating the deepest familial bonds."

I paced, filled with a mix of admiration and regret for Theo Thomas's astrological insights. "It's a pity he's gone. I could have learned so much about star observation from him. I feel a unique sensitivity to these matters."

Flora acknowledged, "Yes, only you and he witnessed the alignment of the seven stars..."

She paused, a puzzled expression crossing her face, before continuing, "I suspect he saw everything in the stars, perhaps even recognizing your unique sensitivity. Maybe he knew you were influenced by a specific star, shaping your thoughts and actions throughout your life."

I nodded enthusiastically, "I always told you I must be a star incarnate, otherwise how could I be so exceptional?"

Flora gave me a skeptical look, "I don't think you're that exceptional, and you're completely wrong about that."

Her words caught me off guard, leaving me momentarily perplexed. I had thought we were on the same page, and her assertion left me questioning.

I waited for her to elaborate, but when she didn't, I pressed, "What do you mean?"

Flora explained slowly, ""The idea of stars descending as incarnations on Earth is a traditional, simplistic notion, not quite aligned with our understanding."

I protested, "But we agreed that many people on Earth are influenced by star power."

She nodded, "Yes, but that's different from 'stars descending as incarnations on   earth.' That phrase implies the person is the star's embodiment, capable of independent thought and action, truly their own master."

Her clarification offered a new dimension to our discussion, suggesting a deeper, more nuanced relationship between celestial influence and human agency. It was a reminder of the complexity of our universe and the mysteries we still had to unravel.

As I listened to Flora's explanation, it slowly began to make sense. I waved my hand, wanting to interject, but she continued, "Being influenced by the stars is quite different.

A person might, due to their unique brain structure, become sensitive to a mysterious energy emitted by a particular star. From that point on, their thoughts and actions could be entirely controlled by this star. They become a slave to it, losing their sense of self, even if they believe otherwise."

I took a deep breath, trying to grasp the concept. "Are you suggesting there's some kind of creature on the star controlling people on Earth?"

Flora shook her head. "It's possible, but more likely, this influence is a natural byproduct of the stars themselves, not the work of a creature. For example, the phases of the moon can affect the emotions of sensitive individuals, and solar flares can cause disruptions on Earth, leading to widespread chaos."

I said, "The moon and the sun are so close to us..." Immediately, I realized the inaccuracy of my words. The moon and the sun are certainly not close to us. The moon is 384,000 kilometers away from Earth, and the sun is even farther, at 150 million kilometers.

When I said they were "close," it was a relative statement, a conclusion drawn by comparing them to other celestial bodies in the universe. Compared to other celestial bodies, they are indeed very close. The distance between the Earth and the sun is only eight minutes for light to travel. In the boundless universe, celestial bodies that are dozens of light years away from Earth are also considered close, and some are even as far as tens of millions of light years. In comparison, the sun is undeniably close.

Flora nodded, understanding my point. "Exactly. The sun's proximity allows it to affect a broad spectrum of people, while distant stars might influence only a select few or even just one person."

Her explanation was straightforward, yet profound. My earlier pride in believing I had a special connection with a star faded away. I wasn't a "star descending to earth," merely someone caught in the star's influence.

Realizing that I was just a slave to a cosmic stone, whose power is exerted unconsciously, was sobering. There was no joy in this revelation, only a sense of loss. Those unaffected by stars, though considered "ordinary," at least retained their autonomy. Meanwhile, those deemed extraordinary might have lost their true selves without even realizing it, taking pride in achievements not entirely their own.

My mood plummeted, and Flora noticed. She sighed softly, "Perhaps none of us truly controls our own fate. Otherwise, how could astrology predict our destinies?"

Her words resonated deeply. It was a humbling thought—that our lives might be influenced by forces beyond our comprehension, shaping our paths in ways we may never fully understand. It made me question the nature of free will and the extent to which we are truly masters of our own destinies.

I paused for a long time before saying, "I am not only saddened by my fate, but I think that the life, thoughts, and behaviors of all human beings on Earth are controlled by different stars. So, what is the meaning of human life?"

Flora spread her hands, looking confused and helpless. She didn't say anything, but I knew she was conveying: That is a question that no one has been able to answer since ancient times.

It's perhaps best not to dwell too deeply on such existential questions. After a moment, Flora broke the silence, "This is the secret of the empty gold-painted box. Without the patience to unlock those intricate chain locks, we would never have uncovered it."

I felt a twinge of embarrassment, realizing that my impatience could have kept Theo Thomas's legacy hidden forever. I raised my hands in a gesture of apology. Flora smiled, suggesting, "We should inform Harlan Brown."

I considered it and replied, "Of course, but let's let him discover it on his own."

Flora nodded in agreement. I rearranged the copper rings, restoring them to their original shapes. True to form, Harlan Brown arrived swiftly, full of energy and urgency. "What did you find? Which city is doomed to disaster?" he demanded.

His question caught us off guard. In our lengthy discussion, we hadn't addressed the immediate concern signaled by the "Seven Stars Linking the Light."

Feeling slightly abashed, I replied, "We haven't tackled that yet. But we did uncover Theo Thomas's secret. Remember the gold-painted box? Flora managed to unlock it fully, and while it seemed empty, the secret was actually in the ring locks."

Harlan Brown, wiping away his sweat, was visibly excited. "What secret?" he pressed.

"You'll have to discover it yourself," I challenged him. "We all figured it out on our own."

Harlan Brown accepted the challenge eagerly but asked, "Any hints?"

I chuckled, "Just recall everything Theo Thomas ever said. It's late, and we need to sleep. Even if you figure it out before we wake, don't disturb us. Everything you need is in the basement."

With a playful whistle, Harlan Brown headed to the basement, while Flora and I retired to the bedroom. Despite the late hour, I opened the window to gaze at the expansive starry sky.

For those skilled in astrology, the sky reveals impending earthly events—great and small. Yet, to the untrained eye, it's merely a canvas of brilliant beauty.

Astrologers, through extensive observation, have established patterns: which celestial conditions presage war, natural disasters, the passing of great leaders, or collective human madness. The rare alignment of the seven stars, in particular, forewarns of a looming catastrophe for a major city.

As I pondered these thoughts, I realized the profound mystery and interconnectivity of the cosmos and our lives, and the balance of knowledge and ignorance we navigate in attempting to understand our place in the universe.

Flora leaned against me, her presence comforting amidst the swirling thoughts. After a while, she whispered, "Go to sleep."

I sighed, feeling the weight of the unknown. "It's odd. Aside from witnessing the strange phenomenon of the seven stars aligning recently, I know so little about astrology."

Flora smiled, her words tinged with mystery. "If everyone could see astrology clearly, what secrets would remain in the world?"

A thought struck me. "Someone like Theo Thomas, with his exceptional ability to read the stars—is he, too, influenced by a particular star?"

"Of course," Flora replied, confirming my suspicion.

I pondered further, trying to organize my jumbled thoughts. "If that's the case, perhaps stars can be categorized as either benevolent or malevolent. The malevolent stars bring disasters—both natural and human-made. Human disasters are often more devastating than natural ones. The thirty stars of the Black Dragon's Seven Constellations, for instance, drove thirty people to unleash great suffering on Earth."

Flora considered this before responding, "Yes, and the benevolent stars counteract those disasters. They influence certain people to advance civilization, knowledge, science, and art."

Feeling more bewildered, I asked, "Then what is Earth? A battlefield for these cosmic forces of good and evil?"

Flora's expression shifted as she proposed an intriguing idea. "I think it's more like a chessboard."

"Chessboard?" I echoed, surprised by her analogy.

"Yes," Flora explained. "A chessboard, with humans as the pieces. Controlled by an incomprehensible force, they wage battles on this board. Victory or defeat holds no real significance for us."

I turned to her, intrigued. "What meaning does it hold for the controlling force itself? You mentioned earlier that this mysterious power might not come from conscious beings but from the stars themselves."

Flora looked as puzzled as I felt. "Who knows," she murmured. "Who knows."

Indeed, who could know? These questions lie far beyond the reach of human understanding. Even as civilizations advance, humanity might never grasp that we are merely pawns on a cosmic chessboard, guided by the enigmatic forces of the stars. No matter one's importance, each person is simply another piece in the grand game.

I was overwhelmed by a profound sadness. Immobilized by the weight of these thoughts, I eventually collapsed onto the bed, sleep eluding me.

As dawn approached, a phrase surfaced in my mind: "Being a pawn crossing the river, I have to move forward desperately."

I drifted into a fitful sleep, burdened by confusion and melancholy. When I finally awoke around noon, Flora was already up.

Exiting the bedroom, we were met by Wilson, the old servant, who approached with a worried expression, speaking in hushed tones. "That Mr. Brown... he's acting strangely."

Alarmed, I listened as Wilson continued, "This morning, I found him in the living room, drenched in sweat. When I asked if he needed anything, he just stared blankly, not responding. It was as if he'd been possessed."

Exchanging a glance with Flora, we hurried downstairs. There, we found Harlan Brown seated on a sofa in the corner, his eyes wide and unseeing, sweat streaming down his face and soaking his hair.

The sight was unsettling, and we realized that whatever he had discovered in the basement had profoundly affected him. The mysteries of the stars and their influence had claimed another mind, and it was up to us to help him find his way back.

I called out urgently, "Harlan Brown."

He seemed to snap out of his trance a bit, though he still didn't meet my gaze, maintaining that vacant, haunted expression Wilson had described as "possessed"

I approached him gently, trying to offer comfort. "Harlan Brown, even if you can't solve the riddles on the copper rings, there's no need to let it trouble you so deeply."

At my words, Harlan Brown snorted and rolled his eyes in a way that suggested he had indeed unraveled Theo Thomas's secret. But if he had solved it, why was he so distressed? His demeanor suggested he was deeply troubled, consumed by anxiety and distress.

It was perplexing. Flora, standing behind me, asked, "Are you feeling unwell?"

Harlan Brown jolted slightly. "No, I'm fine," he replied, standing up with an air of defiance.

Flora and I exchanged startled glances. The sofa where he'd been sitting was soaked, a testament to how long he'd been there and how much he'd been sweating. In such a state, one might even faint. His voice was hoarse as he requested, "Water, give me some water."

I quickly fetched a large glass, which he downed in one go. He wiped his face with his hands, glanced at the wet marks on the sofa, and tried to play it off. "I sweated a lot? Whenever I think deeply about important issues, it happens, since I was a child."

I couldn't help but point out, "Your body's given you away. You're anxious because you don't know what's going on."

Harlan Brown wiped his face again, clearly wrestling with something internally. He finally sighed, "Yes, I am a little worried."

I studied him closely, knowing his temperament—if something was bothering him, he'd usually confide in his friends. This time, however, he looked away, avoiding eye contact, indicating he wasn't ready to share his concerns. We stood at an impasse until I relented, "Okay, if something's on your mind, can you tell your old friend?"

Under normal circumstances, I might have waited for him to open up. But his demeanor was so unlike his usual self that I sensed he might truly need assistance. Friends might tease each other, but we should be there when it counts.

Harlan Brown's body trembled slightly. After a long pause, he spoke, "Ash, even though you might not always like me, I've always seen you as my most respected friend."

His sincerity caught me off guard, leaving me both moved and a bit ashamed. I didn't dislike Harlan Brown, but I hadn't always agreed with his methods, and I'd often teased him. His words made me feel a mix of disturbance and guilt.

"Harlan Brown, if you took any of our differences or jokes to heart, I apologize. Of course, we're good friends."

Hearing this, Harlan Brown turned to me, clasping my hand. His eyes were red, and I noticed his body was trembling slightly. It was clear he was deeply moved, perhaps more than I had realized.

CHAPTER 10

HARLAN'S WEIRD BEHAVIOR

In the dimly lit room, an unsettling silence lingered, punctuated only by the uneven breaths of Harlan Brown. I found myself at a crossroads, unsure of how to proceed. "Take it easy," I urged gently, trying to pierce through the tension. "Let's talk about it."

Harlan Brown appeared on the brink of revelation, but emotion choked his voice, leaving him to utter unintelligible sounds. His eyes, wide with urgency, sought mine for understanding. "We are good friends," I reminded him, my voice steady. "Don't be anxious. Speak slowly."

His grip on my hand tightened, a silent plea that left me seeking Flora's assistance. Her confusion mirrored my own as she attempted to diffuse the situation with a light-hearted tone. "What's wrong with you? Everyone knows you're good friends."

Finally, from the depths of his struggle, Harlan Brown managed to croak out, "Good... friends."

Flora, ever the jester, quipped, "Yes, what happened? It's as if we're staring down the eternal divide between life and death. I'm almost ready to break into 'Auld Lang Syne'."

Her humor was well-placed, a balm to the escalating tension. Yet, despite her efforts, the weight of the moment crushed her levity. Harlan Brown reacted as though struck by an unseen force, recoiling and releasing my hand. His ashen face twisted with an indescribable turmoil.

Flora and I exchanged bewildered glances, caught off-guard by his unpredictable shift. Harlan Brown turned away, bracing himself against the wall. Flora's subtle gesture urged me to remain where I was, allowing him space to regain composure.

After a drawn-out moment, he faced us again, visibly drained but more composed. His voice carried a fatigue that echoed his inner turmoil. "Flora, why are you imitating Ash? It's not funny."

Flora's gentle smile belied her curiosity. "I'm sorry, I didn't mean it. I just wanted to lighten the mood."

His attempt at a smile was a mask, strained and unconvincing. Beneath it lay a deep-seated worry, gnawing at his spirit. In an effort to shift the conversation, Harlan Brown clapped his hands, a forced gesture of camaraderie. "Ash, how long did it take you to solve the secret of the copper ring?"

"It took quite a while," I admitted, recalling the hours spent unraveling the mystery.

Harlan Brown paced, pouring himself a glass of water and downing it in a single gulp. "Yes, you gave me a hint. I didn't waste time on the empty boxes. Theo Thomas's secret was truly a labyrinth only you could navigate."

"This is all Flora's credit," I remarked, acknowledging her pivotal role.

Harlan Brown, ever the philosopher, replied, "Flora solved the secret, but it was because of you. Your presence is like the primer in a Chinese medicinal recipe or the catalyst in a chemical reaction."

His analogy amused me, yet it was not entirely inaccurate. He continued, "Theo Thomas was wise to seek you out. Your influence enabled Flora to unravel the mystery, and I..."

Abruptly, his words halted, leaving an unfinished thought hanging in the air. It was unlike Harlan Brown, a man whose words flowed unceasingly, to stop mid-sentence.

I waited, expecting him to pick up where he left off. Instead, he veered onto a different track. "Those black dots represent thirty people," he explained, "and after various transformations, only seven remain."

Flora and I nodded in unison, and I clapped my hands in acknowledgment. "Indeed, you truly solved Theo Thomas's puzzle."

Harlan Brown fell into a prolonged silence, during which Flora and I shared our own insights from the previous night's revelations. He listened intently, his demeanor composed, offering only nods of agreement without interruption.

Finally, he spoke again, a question lingering in his tone. "Do people not possess their own will? When one chooses to embark on a monumental task, is that decision not their own, but rather the influence of mysterious forces from the stars?"

"Unless Theo Thomas's astrological observations are completely disproven," I replied, "we must entertain the possibility."

A bitter smile crossed Harlan Brown's face, and he waved dismissively, signaling his reluctance to delve deeper into the topic. Flora and I held our tongues, wary of provoking another unexpected reaction.

After a pause, he continued, "Ash, you're aware of the vision of the seven stars, and you understand it foretells the destruction of a great city, yet the specifics elude you."

"Yes," I confessed. "Have you discovered what it signifies?"

Harlan Brown remained silent, prompting me to speculate. "What? Mount Fuji erupting to destroy Tokyo, or perhaps Honolulu buried under volcanic ash?"

His glare was sharp, yet he withheld any further revelation. Rising from his seat, he declared, "I must take my leave. There is much yet to be done."

With that, he extended his hand, first to shake mine, and then Flora's, leaving us with more questions than answers as he departed.

As Harlan Brown shook our hands and made his way to the door, a sense of unease lingered in the air. His behavior was uncharacteristic, raising questions we couldn't quite articulate. When exactly had he started this peculiar ritual of bidding us farewell with such gravity?

At the door, he paused, casting a final glance back at us. I seized the moment, offering, "If you need any help, just come."

His response was an enigmatic laugh, a sound that echoed with layers I couldn't decipher, before he disappeared down the hallway.

Flora and I sat in silence for several moments. "Harlan Brown seems like a different person today," I mused.

Flora nodded thoughtfully. "I suspect he has a significant decision weighing on him."

I sighed, the mystery of his behavior gnawing at me. "This guy..."

Flora interrupted gently, "We should keep a close eye on his actions, see what he's planning."

Under normal circumstances, I might have dismissed his oddities as another of his quirks. But today was different. "Alright," I agreed. "I'll arrange for someone to monitor his movements discreetly."

"That would be wise," Flora concurred.

Over the next three days, I entrusted Steve's private detective agency with the task of shadowing Harlan Brown. Their daily reports left Flora and me more perplexed than before.

The detective's findings were baffling. Harlan Brown had visited a law firm to draft a will. Through a generous bribe, the detective had gleaned its contents, and the revelations were astonishing.

In his will, Harlan Brown appointed me and Flora as executors of his estate upon his death. While this was not entirely unexpected given our friendship, his directive to use his wealth for exploring and researching unexplained phenomena was peculiar, albeit aligned with his lifelong curiosity.

The strangest clause, however, was his self-imposed declaration of death. He stipulated that he would contact the lawyer on a predetermined date, and if he failed to make a second call within thirty days, he should be declared legally deceased.

This was highly irregular. Typically, legal death declarations require a person to be missing for several years, not merely thirty days. Yet, Harlan Brown's insistence turned his will into more of a power of attorney for his estate.

Flora and I exchanged concerned glances as we read through the report. This unexpected twist in his behavior hinted at something deeper, something that lay beyond our understanding.

"What does Harlan Brown want to do?" I pondered aloud, the mystery deepening with every report we received.

Flora's voice was contemplative. "It seems he's preparing for a journey, one that might be fraught with danger."

I groaned in frustration, muttering, "This man is always chasing wild fantasies. Has he discovered aliens and is planning to travel to another planet?"

Flora offered a wry smile. "Stranger things have happened. With him, anything is possible."

I slapped the table decisively. "I need to confront him, find out what he's up to. If he's embarking on some reckless venture, we should at least try to dissuade him."

Flora considered this for a moment. "I fear it won't make a difference. If he wanted to confide in you, he'd already have knocked on your door in the dead of night. If he doesn't want to share, no amount of questioning will change that."

Her words rang true. With a resigned sigh, I returned my attention to the report. One entry caught my eye: Harlan Brown had spent considerable time loitering around a middle school. The school's name was unfamiliar, its location unremarkable.

"What business does he have at a middle school?" I wondered aloud.

Flora speculated, "Perhaps it's his alma mater. People often feel a strong pull towards the places of their youth."

I scoffed, "He's not dying, so why the nostalgic tour?"

Flora's expression turned serious. "Remember how he reacted when I mentioned ' Auld Lang Syne'? Perhaps I inadvertently struck a chord. Whatever decision he's facing, it might be a matter of life and death for him."

Reflecting on Harlan Brown's peculiar behavior, I conceded that Flora's theory held weight, though I struggled to accept it. "What, does he think he's sacrificing himself for some noble cause? There's no great war or epic battle. Is he planning to join some distant conflict?"

Flora shook her head. "I can't decipher it either, but his resolve is undeniable."

That evening, I called him, hoping to glean some insight into his plans. Our conversation, however, yielded little except confirmation that the middle school was indeed his alma mater.

The next day's report left us both stunned. Harlan Brown had visited his parents' grave, paying homage in a solemn ritual that suggested he was preparing to close a chapter of his life.

The pieces were falling into place, yet the picture remained incomplete, an enigma that challenged our understanding and left us grasping for answers.

Harlan Brown's recent actions were increasingly alarming. His visit to his parents' gravesite seemed like a poignant farewell, hinting at the gravity of his intentions. Although I never knew him to be particularly filial, this gesture suggested a deeper, more personal journey was afoot.

Upon his return, he spent the day meeting various people, only to end it alone at a bar, drowning his thoughts in alcohol and mingling with strangers. It was as if he were tying up loose ends or saying his goodbyes.

The third day brought revelations that demanded intervention. Harlan Brown's activities were now beyond peculiar—they were dangerous. That morning, surveillance captured him making a series of phone calls from home. Thanks to Steve's full-tracking measures, including a bug on his home phone, we received a recording of one call that stood out.

As Flora and I listened, the conversation unfolded between Harlan Brown and a woman with a gentle yet unsettlingly charming voice.

Harlan: Last night, I finally got this phone number in a bar.

Female voice: Yes, what advice do you have?

Harlan: (hesitant) Did I...did I dial the wrong number? Or was I misled? I expected a cold man's voice.

Female voice: (with a sweet chuckle) You've watched too many movies, sir. Reality often defies cinematic expectations. You have the right number.

Harlan: (breathing deeply) Alright, I understand you have a price.

Female voice: Sir, everyone has a price.

Harlan: My situation is unique. I wish to meet you.

Female voice: (turning icy) Repeat that request, and you'll face death.

Harlan: (quickly) Please understand, I'm sincere. I need something... perhaps some sophisticated tools from your line of work. I'm willing to pay any price.

Female voice: (pausing) What tools?

Harlan: The most effective ones that can bypass strict inspections. They must be foolproof.

Female voice: I can supply them, but we won't meet. The price is $300,000.

Harlan: (without hesitation) Agreed. I'll have the cash ready. How will we make the exchange?

Female voice: Go to the airport public telephone No. 30 for further instructions.

Harlan: (repeatedly) Yes. Yes. Thank you.

The call concluded ominously. Afterward, Harlan Brown headed straight to a bank, emerging with a suitcase—likely containing the $300,000 in cash—and made his way to the airport.

As Harlan Brown loitered near the public phone, his anxiety was palpable. Every time someone approached the booth, his tension rose, especially when a burly man almost escalated the situation into a confrontation. For three long hours, he lingered, making futile calls that went unanswered, frustration mounting with each ring.

Then, unexpectedly, an old woman in a wheelchair, guided by a little girl, approached the phone. The girl asked Harlan Brown to exchange a banknote for coins. Initially impatient, something in their brief exchange shifted his demeanor entirely. His face softened, and he handed over the coins, departing the phone booth in apparent satisfaction. It was the little girl he had been waiting for—a contact more inconspicuous than anticipated.

Harlan Brown then drove to the bank, his earlier suitcase noticeably absent when he reemerged. The time spent in the manager's office remained a mystery, an enigma that the tracking team couldn't penetrate. Once home, he didn't venture out again, leaving Flora and me with more questions than answers.

Flora broke the silence first. "Harlan Brown is involved with a secret organization."

I couldn't help my skepticism. "He's playing a dangerous game. I'm convinced his contact is a top-tier assassin."

Flora raised an eyebrow, considering the implications. "What puzzles me is that he isn't hiring the killer to eliminate someone. He just wants the tools. Is he planning to commit murder himself?"

"It certainly seems that way," I replied gravely. "I need to confront him before he spirals further into this madness."

The urgency was clear. Harlan Brown was entangled in something perilous, and it was time to intervene and pull him back before he crossed a line from which there was no return.

Flora's words lingered in my mind as I drove to Harlan Brown's home. "We are going to stop him, but he may not be fooling around. Maybe he is preparing to do something big," she had said, and I couldn't shake the feeling that she might be right. Still, the uncertainty gnawed at me.

When I arrived at his large, echoing house, memories of my previous stays there—particularly those spent studying a soul trapped in charcoal—flooded back. I rang the doorbell and pounded on the door with mounting impatience. After several unanswered attempts and a few kicks, the door swung open abruptly, and I nearly collided with Harlan Brown.

He was taken aback. "What shameful things are you doing?" I demanded, my voice laced with suspicion. "Why didn't you come to open the door for so long?"

"I'm sorry," he stammered, "I was in the bathroom... upstairs. I didn't hear the bell."

I wasn't convinced. He could have claimed he was on the roof, and I still wouldn't have believed him. I pushed past him into the house, prompting his protest, "Hey, this is my home!"

I spun around, pointing at him with a resolve that brooked no argument. "For the time being. But remember, I have full authority to dispose of this house after you die or if there's no news from you for 30 days. I'm just getting acquainted with it early."

The tactic worked; his reaction was immediate. His face fell, and he muttered something about the law firm needing more discreet employees.

"You should know there are no true secrets in this world," I pressed, watching his expression change from flustered to defiant.

"Yes," he declared, his voice gaining strength. "I dare say my actions are a secret. You have no idea what I'm planning, and no matter what you do, I won't tell you!"

I had to admit, I was in the dark about his plans. But I couldn't show it. I feigned confidence, hoping to rattle him. "If you don't want others to know, then don't do it yourself. Harlan Brown, you don't even have a one in ten thousand chance of success."

His shock was visible but fleeting, quickly replaced by a sneer. "His shock was visible but fleeting, quickly replaced by a sneer. "Ash, you can't scare me with such words. Go home and continue with your mundane life."

His words stung, not because they were true, but because they were a reminder of the stakes involved. Whatever Harlan Brown was planning, it was dangerous, and his defiance only made me more determined to uncover the truth and stop him before it was too late.

I felt a twinge of embarrassment as I softened my approach. "Alright, whatever you're planning, as a good friend, I only have one piece of advice: don't do it. You've already put yourself in a precarious situation. Don't take another step forward, or you'll regret it."

Harlan Brown met my gaze, his eyes unreadable. He paced briefly, then kicked aside a few large cushions scattered on the floor before settling into a sofa. "It's useless," he said, enunciating each word with quiet firmness. "I won't listen."

Frustrated, I mirrored his actions, angrily kicking away a few cushions before sitting opposite him. "Do you understand the consequences of dealing with professional killers?"

He waved dismissively, his tone nonchalant. "It's really nothing."

His cavalier attitude in the face of such danger was staggering. Professional killers don't just fulfill contracts—they also eliminate threats to their secrecy. His indifference only confirmed Flora's theory: Harlan Brown was prepared to risk everything, even his life, for whatever he was planning.

I sighed, a bitter smile tugging at my lips. "All these years, I never imagined you'd be so willing to sacrifice yourself."

His response was unexpectedly spirited. Though he quickly regained composure, his voice was steady. "It's nothing. Everyone must do something meaningful in their life."

Before I could reply, he chuckled, a hint of irony in his voice. "Perhaps my actions aren't entirely my own. Maybe I'm merely a pawn of the cosmos, influenced by some distant planet. So no matter what you say, my path remains unchanged."

His words amused and baffled me, yet they underscored his resolve. He had blocked every avenue of persuasion, leaving me with the uncomfortable understanding that he was committed to his course.

I ventured further, trying to appeal to reason. "Harlan Brown, you're incredibly talented, but killing isn't your forte. It's not just about having sophisticated tools."

He sprang up, his face paling, before sinking back down. "You're despicable," he muttered, realizing that I had been tracking him.

I held his gaze, speaking earnestly. "We're friends, aren't we? I wouldn't have bothered if it were anyone else."

His forced smile faded into a proud defiance. "You still don't know what I'm planning."

I admitted, "True. Otherwise, I wouldn't be here, trying to understand."

His shoulders relaxed, and he let out a long breath. "That's great, that's great."

In that moment, I realized that while I might not have changed his mind, I had at least opened a channel of communication. Perhaps there was still a chance to uncover his intentions and guide him away from the precipice.

Realizing my initial approach wasn't working, I shifted tactics. "I'm more experienced with sophisticated weapons than you are. Why don't you show me what you've got? I might be able to offer some advice."

Harlan Brown's pride was evident. "If I wanted to kill you, you'd already be cold."

It was then that I noticed the ring on his finger, a design I'd never seen before. Its flat, silver surface was engraved with simple patterns, innocuous enough to escape notice.

I gestured towards it, and Harlan Brown nodded, confirming my suspicion.

"It's not easy to hit a target with that," I remarked.

He shook his head. "It has an effective range of ten meters."

A chill ran through me. Harlan Brown was serious about this. What could have driven him to such a drastic decision?

I forced a bitter smile. "Does it shoot a needle?"

He nodded.

"And the needle is poisoned, I assume. What's the toxin?"

"It's extracted from the skin of a South American tree frog," he replied.

I clenched my fists. "If true, that toxin can cause heart paralysis and death in three seconds."

"Exactly," he confirmed.

I sighed, trying to dissuade him. "You might have spent $300,000 on a toy. Sure, it shoots a needle, but it might not have the poison you think."

Harlan Brown smiled. "The transaction is fair. The money is in a Swiss bank, only to be released once I confirm the poison's efficacy."

His explanation left me speechless. "That's... remarkably fair. But what if something goes wrong during your 'operation'?"

"They have a deadline. If I don't report back, they can still take the money. As long as I'm within ten meters, I can raise my hand and—"

He lifted his hand towards me in demonstration, and I instinctively grabbed a cushion, holding it defensively.

Harlan Brown laughed, clearly enjoying my reaction.

Despite the seriousness of his intentions, his conviction that he was in the right was unsettling. He genuinely believed in the righteousness of his actions, which only deepened the mystery around his motives. I needed to understand what he planned to do and why he was willing to go to such lengths, but I also knew that time was running out to stop him.

CHAPTER 11

HARLAN'S MAJOR DISCOVERIES

Frustration welled up inside me. "I've never seen anyone so pleased with the idea of taking a life," I said, my annoyance barely concealed.

Harlan Brown's laughter ceased, and his expression turned grave. "Are you accusing me?"

I waved my hand dismissively, trying to avoid a confrontation. "Not accusing, just curious. I'm trying to understand your mindset. You've decided to kill someone and seem committed to it. How does that feel?"

My question was more than curiosity; it was a probe for clues. I needed to uncover who his target was.

His gaze was unyielding, devoid of remorse. He scrutinized me, his silence stretching on. His eyes held a peculiar quality, as if he pitied me. Under his stare, I felt my initial advantage slip away.

I shifted uncomfortably. "You haven't answered my question."

He spoke slowly, deliberately. "I won't answer now. You'll understand once I've acted. It's not about my mindset; it's the influence of the stars. They compel me."

I pressed further, "Is this related to the secret Theo Thomas left on the copper ring?"

His peculiar behavior had begun after that night in my basement, studying the copper rings. But he merely pressed his lips together, refusing to confirm or deny.

I tried every tactic I could think of—questions both direct and subtle, softly spoken or shouted in frustration. I even resorted to waving my fists or standing in exasperation. Yet, he remained impassive, responding only with irritating sneers or silence.

Finally, I slumped back in my seat, defeated. "Don't waste your energy," he said coldly. "Go back to sleep."

"Do you really think I'll just stop here?" I snapped, anger flaring.

He sneered again. "And what will you do? Keep sending people to follow me?"

His words stung, but they sparked an idea. Perhaps the answer wasn't in confronting him directly. As I considered my options, a plan began to form in my mind. I needed a different approach, something unconventional that might unravel the mystery of his intentions and stop him before it was too late.

Harlan Brown's newfound awareness of being followed meant that sending detectives after him again would likely be futile. He was clever and nimble enough to evade them if he chose to. Yet, I played into his expectations, casually declaring, "Of course, I'll continue sending people to follow you."

He chuckled, clearly amused by the prospect. "Alright, let's see if your hound can catch me."

I laughed along, masking my true intentions. I had a different plan in mind, one that didn't rely on traditional surveillance. When he boldly suggested I leave, I took a moment, standing up slowly and speaking earnestly. "You shouldn't see me as an enemy. I came here sincerely wanting to help. When Flora and I deduced your intention to kill, we believed you had your reasons. But you've shut me out."

My words, though simple, seemed to resonate with him. He paused, visibly moved before responding with a sigh, "You are really stupid."

His bluntness caught me off guard, frustrating and perplexing me. Yet, his next words hinted at something deeper. "I called you fool because there's a crucial piece you're missing."

"Then tell me," I urged.

His laughter was both teasing and enigmatic. "I want you to remain in the dark."

Despite my long acquaintance with Harlan Brown, I found myself at a loss. Nevertheless, I had other plans in motion, so I feigned defeat. "Alright, then I can only wish you success."

He surprised me by shaking my hand with enthusiasm, his grip firm and sincere. It was an odd gesture, one that left me guessing at his true intentions.

As he escorted me to the door, waving as I departed, I couldn't shake the feeling of an impending farewell, reminiscent of Flora's words about " Auld Lang Syne."

Turning to face him once more, I felt compelled to caution him. "You know, if you kill someone, you might also be killed. The odds are equal."

His calm reply was unsettling. "I know."

He continued, acknowledging the gravity of his situation. "I know the odds of my being killed are much higher."

I sighed, pressing him one last time. "Why refuse my help? I'm better equipped to handle danger than you are."

He dismissed my offer with a turn of his back, muttering "stupid" once again as he went inside.

Twice he had called me that, and despite the sting, it only fueled my determination. Whatever he was planning, I had to find a way to intervene, even if it meant outsmarting him at his own game.

I watched Harlan Brown disappear into his house and felt the weight of the situation pressing down on me. With no other choice, I headed back to my car, drove around the corner, and parked where I couldn't be seen from his house. I needed a plan, so I ducked into a nearby coffee shop and called Flora.

"We need to keep an eye on Harlan Brown around the clock," I told Flora urgently. "Bring the tracking equipment. We have to do this ourselves so he won't catch on. He's decided to kill someone, but I have no idea who."

Flora agreed without hesitation. "I'll meet you at the corner near his house."

After our call, I walked cautiously back toward Harlan Brown's house. The glow of a light in his studio window was a reassuring sign that he hadn't left yet. I waited patiently until Flora arrived, equipment in hand.

"He answered when I called to check if you had left," Flora said, confirming Harlan's presence at home.

I relayed the details of my encounter with Harlan Brown, including his troubling insistence on calling me "stupid." Flora pondered this. "Why did he call you that? There must be something we're missing."

"Exactly," I agreed. "What could it be?"

Flora considered for a moment. "Do you get the sense that, despite planning to kill someone, he believes his actions are noble?"

"Yes," I replied. "He seems to see it as a sacrifice."

Flora continued, "He paid a hefty price for those weapons. He's planning an assassination."

I nodded. "If it were an open confrontation, I doubt he'd have the nerve."

Flora glanced at the lighted window. "He knows the risks. Whoever he's targeting must be someone heavily guarded—someone significant."

Her analysis hit me hard. The implications were staggering, terrifying even.

"He's on a suicide mission," I murmured. "Even if he succeeds, if his target is a political or military leader, he'll never escape."

"That's why deciding was so painful for him," Flora said softly.

I raised my hand in realization. "The copper ring—after he read its secret—"

In that moment, Flora and I reached the same chilling conclusion. Under the dim streetlight, the gravity of our realization washed over us, leaving us both visibly shaken.

Flora was a few seconds ahead of me. Both of us knew exactly who Harlan Brown was targeting.

This madman, a complete lunatic with no chance of success!

Harlan Brown couldn't possibly get close to his intended target, and the consequences would be dire, possibly worse than death.

My voice trembled slightly. "No, we must stop him."

Flora gestured for me to hold back. "But we still don't know why he's doing this."

I groaned in frustration. "He's crazy. Who knows why he does anything?"

Flora murmured, "There must be a reason."

Ignoring her, I strode to the door, ringing the bell and knocking urgently, shouting Harlan Brown's name.

Flora approached, frowning. "You're making too much noise. You'll wake the neighbors."

I paused momentarily, then continued ringing the bell. Five minutes passed without an answer. I felt something was wrong. I signaled to Flora, opened the small bag she had brought, and took out the lock-picking tools. Quickly unlocking the door, I pushed it open and shouted, "Harlan Brown."

Flora followed me in, and we entered the lit room. It was Harlan Brown's studio, filled with all manner of instruments and strange equipment, which he had set up for contact with aliens, communication with souls, and various other peculiar purposes he had imagined.

In the center of the room, a large table held a sheet of paper with two lines of bold handwriting. Even from a distance, I recognized Harlan Brown's unmistakable script, brimming with excitement and perhaps a hint of mockery. The words read: "Ash, I know you will follow me personally. As soon as you leave from the front door, I will slip away from the back door, haha! haha!"

Stunned, I immediately instructed, "We need to stop him from leaving the country."

Flora offered a rueful smile. "He could leave by land, sea, or air. How can we intercept him?"

"Do everything we can," I insisted.

I grabbed the phone, waking up Steve to mobilize all detectives to cover every possible exit point. The directive was clear: if they saw Harlan Brown, they should stop him by any means necessary, even if it meant breaking his legs.

For the next two hours, I tried every avenue to prevent his escape. It became apparent, however, that Harlan Brown hadn't left through legal channels. I speculated he might be lying low for a while before making his move. I asked Flora to return home while I kept watch at Harlan Brown's place. Days turned into weeks, and after half a month with no sign of him, my worry deepened.

During those two weeks, I cursed his recklessness countless times. As time passed, I feared he had either perished during his assassination attempt or was captured, subjected to relentless interrogation. Given the target Flora and I suspected, any successful attack would have sent shockwaves around the globe. The absence of such news suggested his failure.

From the fifth day, I sensed his dire fate. I reached out through various channels, probing for any information. But given the indirect nature of these connections, concrete answers were elusive. After a fortnight, I convened with Flora, agreeing that one of us needed to pursue this lead in person.

To my surprise, Flora volunteered, saying, "If someone has to go, I'll go."

Flora's determination was palpable as she spoke. "I don't want you to be caught up in this mess."

"I want to bring Harlan Brown back," I replied, my voice firm with conviction.

"You're too conspicuous," Flora countered. "Your movements wouldn't go unnoticed by any intelligence agency."

I scoffed, "I can evade any spy organization on this planet."

With a sigh, Flora pressed on, "Let me go first, okay?"

I met her gaze, recognizing the validity in her suggestion. Reluctantly, I nodded.

She smiled softly, then asked, "Why do you think Harlan Brown is doing this? Any thoughts?"

"He's lost his mind," I said, my frustration evident.

But Flora shook her head. "There has to be a reason. It's odd that he saw something in those copper rings that we didn't. Our analytical skills are on par with his, yet he was compelled to act."

"Maybe because we're not crazy," I muttered under my breath.

Flora shot me a look. "Think back over everything Harlan Brown said and did. You're familiar with him, his mindset. There might be a clue in his words or actions."

I nodded, acknowledging her point. As she prepared to leave, she reassured me, "I'll keep in touch."

Watching her drive away filled me with unease. She was right—if Harlan Brown had acted, it would stir international chaos. The implications were vast, and the potential fallout was frightening. I couldn't shake the feeling of helplessness, knowing that the situation was fraught with danger.

I couldn't help but reflect on the irony of the situation. The complexities of human ignorance and darkness felt more daunting than any natural danger. While I could face physical threats with courage, the entanglements of human conflict and misunderstanding were a different kind of peril altogether. With Flora on her way to untangle the mystery, I resolved to piece together any clues I could from Harlan Brown's past actions and words.

I would rather take my chances in the black forests of Africa than go there to inquire about someone's news. The irony is striking. Human beings can embody such willful ignorance and darkness, more terrifying and suffocating than any primeval forest.

My thoughts were in disarray. About half an hour later, the doorbell rang unexpectedly.

Opening the door, I found a middle-aged woman with a strong rural accent, her appearance nondescript, carrying luggage. She asked, "Is Mr. Wright home?" showing me a letter with an address.

Realizing she had the wrong place, I directed her across the street. "You're at the wrong address. It's over there."

I watched the woman struggle with her luggage, thanked me, and headed across the street. I didn't give her another thought as I returned inside, intent on following Flora's advice to review everything about Harlan Brown's recent behavior.

Leaning back on the sofa, I heard a "rustling" sound. Sitting up straight, I reached behind me and felt a piece of paper stuck to my back!

I was utterly taken aback - Ash, how could someone play such a prank on you without you noticing?

This kind of joke—a game among elementary school students—where you draw a big turtle on paper and stick it on someone's back unnoticed. Middle school students have long abandoned such antics, yet here I was, a grown adult, with paper stuck to my back.

I immediately recalled the country woman who had asked, "Is Mr. Wright home?"

In that instant, everything clicked, and my nerves gave way to amusement. I reached behind and peeled off the paper. It read: "Look, I know how to hide myself."

It dawned on me that the "country woman" had been Flora in disguise, demonstrating her ability to blend in seamlessly. Her makeup and demeanor had been flawless, leaving no room for suspicion. I couldn't help but admire her skill, even as I chuckled at being so easily duped. Confident in my own ability to disguise myself, I recognized the difficulty of appearing so authentically as a country person.

Slowly folding the paper, I leaned back on the sofa and delved once more into contemplating Harlan Brown's words and actions from beginning to end.

Folding the paper, I leaned back on the sofa, contemplating Harlan Brown's actions. Despite my best efforts, I couldn't divine his ultimate motive. He seemed driven by a sense of purpose, believing his plan was noble. But why the assassination? And why call me "stupid" twice when I was only trying to help?

Frustrated by the lack of clarity, I decided I'd overstayed at Harlan Brown's house. Before leaving, I penned a note on a fresh piece of paper: "See the letter, contact immediately no matter what, otherwise, hehe." I hoped he would eventually return and find it.

As I left, I sighed, thinking of Flora's journey. Her skills were impressive, but the unknowns of her mission weighed heavily on my mind.

Upon arriving home, Wilson opened the door, his expression mischievous. It was clear Flora had confided in him about her prank. "I was fooled," I admitted, meeting his amused gaze.

Wilson grinned. "She really did look the part, didn't she?"

Thinking of Flora's situation brought a brief smile to my face, but as I headed upstairs, my eyes lingered on the basement door. Suddenly, I remembered Harlan Brown's breakthrough with the copper rings. Perhaps retracing his steps would yield some clues.

I ventured down to the basement and was immediately taken aback by what I saw. Since the day I found Harlan Brown drenched in sweat, neither Flora nor I had returned here. But now, the space was different. Nine groups of copper rings lay neatly on the table, which was expected given Harlan's efforts to decode their mystery. What was unexpected were the numerous crumpled pieces of paper strewn across the table and floor, evidence of Harlan Brown's intense thought process.

I picked up one of the papers and flattened it. It bore Harlan's hasty handwriting: "Seven stars connected by rays of light symbolize the destruction of a big city. The following can be confirmed:

1. This big city is in the east; 2. This big city was destroyed due to the destruction of some kind of force. 3.???"

It was clear he had been jotting down his thoughts to facilitate his reasoning. With over 30 such papers around, they were a window into Harlan's mind during those crucial hours in the basement. Had we examined these earlier, we might have understood his motivations sooner.

I quickly gathered all the papers, spreading them out to decipher his scrawled notes. Most covered ground we'd already discussed, but a select few were illuminating. I sorted them, deduced their sequence, and numbered them. Six in total, they laid bare the rationale behind Harlan Brown's bizarre behavior and his drastic decision. Realization hit me hard, and I cursed myself for being so blind. Harlan had been right to call me a fool.

His notes, though chaotic, revealed a truth I had missed. Some words were nearly illegible, but context guided my understanding. I knew I had to act immediately, even if just to bring Flora back.

I dashed out of the basement, startling Wilson, though he merely watched, accustomed to my unpredictable actions. I swiftly transformed my appearance, using makeup and medicated baths to darken and roughen my skin, hacking my hair short. Such a thorough disguise required several hours.

When I descended the stairs again, Wilson gaped at my transformation. "What?" I

asked, impatience creeping into my voice.

He shook his head in disbelief. "What are you up to?"

I sighed, knowing it would be futile to explain. "Even if I told you, you wouldn't understand."

With that, I left. Procuring fake IDs and documents was straightforward; I had contacts who specialized in such things. Once aboard the plane, I exhaled, relieved to be on my way.

As I closed my eyes on the plane, my mind kept turning over Harlan Brown's meticulous reasoning, laid bare on those six pieces of paper. Despite thinking him a lunatic, I couldn't deny that his insights were ones Flora and I hadn't considered.

The first paper, which I found near the door, outlined his initial thoughts: the destruction of a major city and the mysterious "Seven Stars in One" phenomenon. The second paper delved deeper. Harlan Brown wrote:

"Theo Thomas asked Ash to save this disaster. A big city is going to be destroyed. No matter how capable Ash is, what ability can he have to save it?"

This posed a question we had often debated. But Harlan Brown diverged from my skepticism; he held an unwavering belief in Theo Thomas's prophecy:

"Since Theo Thomas said that Ash can save it, he must be able to save it, and it must be confirmed.

The factors that lead to the destruction of a city are:

1. Earthquake or tsunami;

2. Volcanic eruption;

3. Nuclear war;

4. Meteor impact;

5. Plague - impossible in modern times;

6. ...

Ash is unable to save them, there must be another reason."

The third paper was filled with diagrams, composed of points and lines. To the untrained eye, they might appear cryptic, but I recognized them immediately as representations of "Seven Stars in One." I had described the phenomenon to Harlan Brown, showing him the star map and detailing the stars' positions, and his drawings were remarkably accurate.

In his sketches, the convergence of the seven stars formed a small circle. He had drawn it over ten times before annotating:

"It looks like a dragon, about to devour something."

This imagery resonated with me; I, too, had visualized such a simulation when contemplating the phenomenon.

Harlan Brown's fixation on the prophecy and the celestial alignment hinted at something beyond mere destruction. His belief that a solution lay hidden within these symbols suggested a deeper meaning or a hidden mechanism at play. As I pondered these thoughts, I realized that Harlan Brown's actions, however drastic, were rooted in a desperate attempt to prevent an impending catastrophe—a catastrophe he felt uniquely compelled to avert.

As the plane hummed softly, I resolved to parse through the remaining notes once more, hoping to glean further insight into Harlan Brown's mind and the potential path forward. Whatever madness drove him, it was clear he believed he was acting for a greater good, and understanding that could be key to unraveling this mystery.

The revelation from Harlan Brown's notes was profound and chilling. The imagery of the seven stars forming a dragon, with its mouth at the gathering point, suggested a city poised for destruction. Harlan's leap of logic—that this point might represent a specific city—was a perspective I hadn't considered.

Yet, even if we could pinpoint the city, what could be done to prevent its demise?

On the fourth paper, Harlan's trembling lines indicated a moment of intense realization. The seven black dots he drew matched the positions in the smallest copper rings, representing seven individuals influenced by the stars. The similarity between these dots and the star alignment was striking.

Harlan Brown's insight was clear in his shaky handwriting: "How similar are the positions of the seven black dots to the seven stars in convergence?"

This comparison led to a stunning conclusion on the fifth paper. In wild scrawl, Harlan wrote about the stars influencing these seven individuals, leading them to act as if under a spell. The seven people, driven by the stars, had the potential to cause the city's destruction—not through natural calamities, but through their actions, misguided and ignorant.

"To destroy a big city, it is not necessarily a natural disaster, but also a man-made disaster," Harlan wrote. "Man-made disasters are not necessarily wars. A few words from a few people, a few people's ignorant actions, can make a big city completely dead."

My hands trembled as I realized the implications. Our focus on catastrophic events like earthquakes or wars had blinded us to the subtlety of human influence. Harlan's notes suggested that the very fabric of a city's existence could unravel through the misguided deeds of a few.

I recalled a conversation about a gold rush town in the western United States, thriving until its resources were depleted, leaving it a ghost town. At the time, I dismissed it as a quaint anecdote. Now, it was a metaphor for the vulnerability of even the most robust cities.

The realization that even a thriving metropolis could become a hollow shell, bereft of its essence due to the reckless actions of a few, was chilling. The framework of a city—the buildings, the infrastructure—could remain intact, yet the life that fueled it could evaporate, leaving only a facade. This was the true danger foreseen by the "Seven Stars Linked" phenomenon, and it had already begun.

Standing amidst these revelations, I felt a profound sadness for humanity. Throughout history, individuals have emerged, believing themselves capable of altering the course of human destiny. Yet, unbeknownst to them, they were merely instruments of some enigmatic cosmic force, manipulated by the stars' influence.

These individuals, thinking themselves superior, were blind to the reality that every ordinary person could see. They were slaves to an unfathomable power, their actions driven by something beyond their understanding.

This delusion has repeated throughout history, from conquerors like Alexander the Great and Genghis Khan to tyrants like Napoleon and Hitler. Each believed they could command the world, yet each was a mere pawn in a cosmic game.

Why Theo Thomas believed I could alter this course was a mystery. What power did he think I possessed that could counteract the influence of these misguided individuals? Even if I were endowed with the mythical powers of a "Superman," how could I possibly redirect the actions of those blinded by rebellion and ignorance?

I felt a sense of futility. Perhaps Theo Thomas had overestimated my ability to intervene, erring in his judgment.

Harlan Brown seemed to share this sentiment. On the sixth piece of paper, he scribbled numerous words and sentences. The first read:

"Theo Thomas was wrong. Although he knew everything and understood what would happen, no one, including Ash, could stop what will happen."

Following those lines, he filled the page with seventy or eighty question marks, varying in size, a testament to his chaotic thoughts.

Then, he wrote it dozens of times:

He likened the influence of the stars to a controller manipulating a robot. The stars, as controllers, exerted their influence over individuals, the "robots," who acted under this unseen power. The analogy was powerful: a robot, devoid of autonomy, responds solely to the controller's signals. If the robot is destroyed, the controller's influence becomes meaningless, as there's no entity left to manipulate.

I couldn't help but admire Harlan Brown's idea.

Harlan Brown's next logical step was chilling in its simplicity: "No one has the power to change the star, that is, no one can destroy the controller, so the only way is to destroy the controlled robot!"

This line of reasoning revealed his drastic conclusion—that the only way to break the cycle of influence was to eliminate those under the stars' control. It was a stark reflection of his desperation and the lengths he was willing to go to prevent the catastrophe he envisioned.

I felt a wave of admiration for Harlan Brown's bold thinking but also a deep unease at the implications. His willingness to resort to such extreme measures underscored the gravity of the situation as he saw it. His belief was that by removing the controlled individuals, the chain of events leading to the city's destruction could be severed.

This realization brought a sense of urgency. If Harlan Brown was intent on following through with his plan, it was imperative to find him before he acted. His solution, while logical in his framework, was fraught with moral and ethical dilemmas. The potential loss of life was staggering, and the consequences of his actions could be as devastating as the disaster he sought to prevent.

I needed to reach Flora and share these insights. Together, we had to find a way to intercept Harlan Brown and explore alternatives to avert the impending disaster without resorting to irreversible actions. The stakes were higher than ever, and time was of the essence.

Harlan's mind churned with thoughts that defied the ordinary. To him, it wasn't about killing people; it was about dismantling the "robots" and halting the insidious tide of rebellion and ignorance that threatened to spill forth through their artificial forms.

As he scribbled furiously on the sixth sheet of paper, his pen echoed the gravity of his thoughts: "Theo Thomas is right; Ash Morris possesses the capability. But why does he remain oblivious to the disaster's origin and its containment? The truth is undeniable—through Ash, this burden rests squarely on my shoulders."

A series of question marks, each more erratic than the last, punctuated his writing, revealing the storm of contradictions raging within him.

When I encountered this, a bitter smile tugged at my lips. Harlan Brown and Theo Thomas had overestimated me. Assassination was a realm foreign to my talents, repulsive even. And even if I unraveled the entire enigma, the thought of "destroying the robots" would never be my course of action.

Yet, what he contemplated next stirred something deep within me.

"Don't let Ash go. This is a battle where life hangs by a thread, and victories are scarce. Ash—a man with a loving wife and cherished by all his friends. Let it be me instead. Let me go."

"I'll go!"

Those two words, scrawled in bold, untamed strokes, leapt from the page.

This was the essence of Harlan Brown's thought process, the reason he had labeled me a "fool" when I earnestly offered my assistance twice. He never intended for me to shoulder the peril, acting instead in my stead to shield me from danger. And yet, my desire to aid him remained undeterred. Wasn't that the ultimate folly? It explained the fervor in his farewell, knowing he tread on the cusp of peril. Yet, he also knew if he didn't act, I might.

He, my steadfast friend, would rather brave the storm himself than let me face it.

His decision was not made lightly. The introspection left him drenched in sweat, yet neither Flora nor I truly grasped the depth of his resolve.

Harlan Brown's devotion to his friends was reminiscent of the gallant, romantic chivalry of ancient times—a sentiment both exhilarating and noble.

Caught in the whirlwind of emotions stirred by Harlan Brown's selfless chivalry, I found myself torn. On one hand, his actions, once puzzling, now unfolded with a clarity that was both exhilarating and humbling. Yet, on the other hand, a simmering frustration brewed within me. How could he have concocted such a perilous plan without so much as a word to us?

Had he shared his thoughts, Flora and I would have undoubtedly protested his adventure. Neither Flora nor I would take such risks ourselves.

But perhaps, in his own enigmatic wisdom, he was right. He once likened me to the "primer" in a Chinese medicine prescription, the "catalyst" that ignites chemical change. It was through me that Flora unraveled the initial secrets, and through me that Harlan Brown dared to tackle the deeper mysteries.

Confusion clouded my mind, yet amidst the fog, a decision crystallized with startling clarity: Flora's meeting with Harlan Brown was not enough. I had to go, too. Whether this resolve sprouted from my own volition or was nudged by some unseen force, it mattered little. The imperative was clear—I had to act, and I had to act now.

And so, here I am, seated in this cramped, rickety plane, propelled by determination and an unyielding sense of duty.

CHAPTER 12

JOURNEY TO ANOTHER LAND

The enigma of Harlan Brown's mission gnawed at my thoughts. His intent to "destroy the robot" was clear, yet uncertainty loomed over whether dismantling just one would unravel the intricate web of the "Seven Stars Alliance" phenomenon. The answer was elusive, cloaked in mystery.

Weeks had trickled by since he embarked on his perilous quest, yet the "robot" remained intact. It continued to heed the celestial commands, orchestrating chaos and laying waste to the metropolis with relentless precision.

Equipped with a formidable weapon capable of ending lives within ten meters, Harlan faced an insurmountable challenge—how could he bridge the distance to his target without being detected?

The chilling truth was undeniable: even if he succeeded in getting within range, the likelihood of escaping unscathed was dismally low.

As the incessant chatter of the elderly woman beside me filled the cabin, a resolute decision crystallized in my mind: should Flora and I find Harlan Brown, we must steel ourselves against his entreaties. Our sole course of action would be to leave immediately.

Contacting Flora posed no concern. Our bond transcended the need for conventional communication, even in unfamiliar terrain teeming with strangers. It was Harlan Brown's desperation that troubled me; a man on the brink could be more formidable than any adversary.

Though I appeared to rest during the flight, my mind was a tempest of thoughts, swirling through countless possibilities. Upon landing, I swiftly utilized the most expedient local transport to reach my destination.

My priority was to connect with Flora. We had devised a rudimentary yet effective system of leaving clandestine marks at iconic locations, intelligible only to us.

In Paris, our marks would grace the vicinity of the Eiffel Tower, the Louvre, and the Arc de Triomphe. In London, near the Westminster clock and Buckingham Palace.

Unaware of my arrival, Flora would not have left signs for me. Yet, I clung to the hope that she would recall our pact and seek out the marks I scattered.

I secured lodgings at a modest hotel frequented by travelers, then embarked on my mission, leaving subtle marks at several key sites before returning.

The air of suspicion was palpable, an unspoken tension that pervaded each glance exchanged among strangers. I endeavored to move discreetly, avoiding undue attention.

Yet, curiosity found me. "Is this your first time here? Why linger at the hotel?" an inquisitive voice probed.

Unsure of the speaker's identity, I offered a noncommittal reply, "I'm waiting for a friend."

Further questions followed, met with evasive responses, until the questioner withdrew, their gaze lingering with suspicion.

Back in my room, I had scarcely reclined when the door edged open. A dispassionate face peered in as water was added to the thermos.

With a resigned sigh, I rose once more, leaving the hotel to revisit the markers I had placed.

Hope was a distant companion as I approached the third site—a renowned park adorned with a wall bearing a dragon relief. Yet, to my astonishment, another mark now accompanied the one I had left.

Elated, I scanned my surroundings. Dusk had settled, thinning the crowd to a few Western tourists exclaiming over the architecture. By a large tree stood a middle-aged woman, a young boy at her side.

I nearly called out "Flora!" but hesitated, puzzled by the presence of a child. In that moment, the woman glanced my way, then turned, guiding the boy with her, her back to me.

As she subtly signaled me with a familiar hand gesture behind her back, I couldn't help but let out a silent laugh, berating myself for not recognizing her sooner. Her disguise, complete with a little boy in tow, was flawless—enough to deceive anyone, even me.

Maintaining a discreet distance, we maneuvered through the park. Once we reached the bustling street, she whispered to the boy, who then darted off into the fading light. As the evening shadows deepened, I caught up with her at the crosswalk. Flora eyed me appraisingly, "Your disguise isn't half bad. Why the sudden pursuit? Were you worried?"

I shook my head, urgency in my voice, "No, it's because I've uncovered something significant."

We melted into the crowd, blending seamlessly as I recounted the cryptic notes Harlan Brown had left in the basement. Flora listened intently, her expression shifting from concern to resignation. "Harlan Brown's logic is sound, but his methods are reckless. Destroying one robot won't halt the controller—they'll simply activate another."

Hesitant, I replied, "But Theo Thomas believes I can avert this catastrophe. We ought to trust his insight."

Flora remained silent, her lips pressed tightly together. After a few more steps, she spoke again, "Of course we should trust Theo Thomas. But I am certain Harlan Brown's method isn't the solution he intended."

I let out a bitter chuckle, "And what am I supposed to do? Fly into the heavens and extinguish the starlight from the seven stars that mimic dragons?"

She shot me a knowing glance, "You may not have the power to capture a dragon, but you can certainly pursue this malevolent one."

Confounded, I asked, "Pursue... the evil dragon?"

Flora gestured animatedly, her own thoughts a tangled web. After a pause, she clarified, "What I mean is, we know the dragon's trajectory. Its aim is to consume a metropolis. Our only recourse is to track its movements and alert the world to its every step before it strikes."

Frustration welled up within me as I kicked a crumpled piece of paper down the sidewalk, "And what good will that do? It won't alter the reality."

Flora's sigh seemed to echo the constraints of our situation. "It's the most we can do," she lamented. "The actions of a handful of individuals can't sway the decisions of such a powerful force."

I couldn't help but let out a bitter laugh. "Perhaps our efforts would be better spent trying to make those people understand that their actions are leading to the destruction of a city."

Flora's eyes met mine, filled with a familiar resolve. "Remember, their minds are clouded by the influence of the stars. Unless we can alter that power, changing their minds is futile. Our priority should be to save Harlan Brown. Do you have any special ideas?"

I scanned the bustling streets, the crowd a sea of anonymous faces under the dim glow of streetlights. Finding Harlan Brown amidst this throng seemed a daunting task. "He's a stranger here, likely staying at a hotel. We'll split up and check every possible place. Sooner or later, we'll find him."

Though Flora appeared skeptical of my plan, she nodded in agreement, lacking a better alternative. We resolved to meet daily and continue our search separately. For ten days, we scoured the city, but Harlan Brown remained elusive, and my anxiety grew. Upon meeting Flora that evening, I voiced my fears. "They might have arrested him without any public announcement. How can we locate him?"

After a moment's thought, Flora proposed a new strategy. "Let's try for three more days. Instead of searching aimlessly, we'll leave messages in every hotel, asking Harlan Brown to contact us. We'll include our names so he knows it's us, regardless of his disguise or assumed identity."

Her plan risked exposing us, but we had no other options. Besides, we weren't so significant that people would recognize or care about us. For the next three days, we executed Flora's plan. On the third night, as we reconvened, two men approached us. Their demeanor immediately set them apart as anything but ordinary.

One, with a crew cut, fixed us with a cold stare. "Are you searching for someone named Harlan Brown?"

I nodded, my breath catching slightly.

The other man's voice was even more unsettling. "You two are together, yet staying in different hotels and meeting at a set time each day."

It was clear we had been under surveillance. One of the men flashed an ID in front of me. "You'll need to come with us."

I glanced at Flora, seeking her opinion. The men tensed, exchanging whispers. "Don't think about resisting."

Flora's slow nod signaled her agreement to comply. As they urged us along, I remarked, "Looks like we're being taken in."

The men smirked. The one with short hair replied, "Not yet, but you must come with us."

Feigning nonchalance, I shrugged. They flanked us as we walked, and suddenly, several more individuals materialized, hemming us in. A small truck pulled up, and we were ushered inside. Once aboard, a canvas tarp was drawn over the truck bed. We sat on benches opposite four others.

Repeated inquiries about our destination were met with silence, so I fell quiet, contemplating our predicament and the unknown journey ahead.

After a tense half-hour drive, the truck came to a halt in a sprawling compound, stark and industrial, with its expanse of gray cement floors and walls. We were ushered into a room where we waited in silence until two men, clearly of substantial authority, entered. They remained silent, assessing us, until a third man joined them, his presence commanding attention.

Without preamble, he asked, "Are you looking for Harlan Brown?"

I nodded, anticipating this line of inquiry. "He's a close friend," I explained, "and unfortunately, he's mentally ill. He's prone to doing inexplicable things. In another setting, it might not be a big issue, but here, it could lead to serious trouble. We want to find him before he gets himself into a dire situation."

The man scrutinized my response. "Mentally ill? Is that your honest assessment?"

"Yes," I insisted, choosing my words carefully. "His condition is quite severe. He believes he's capable of making significant changes."

The man's laughter was dry, almost cynical. "Indeed, his actions suggest as much."

His expression shifted, becoming more severe. "Our preliminary investigation shows his background is quite complex."

I shifted uneasily, while Flora interjected, "Has he been detained?"

After a pause, the man nodded. Anxiety gripped me, but Flora's subtle signal calmed me. "May I ask why he was arrested?"

"For speaking nonsense," the man replied tersely.

Relief washed over me—Harlan Brown hadn't yet acted on his plans. "In this place, one must be cautious about what they say," I remarked.

The man's demeanor darkened further. "He masqueraded as a reporter..."

I interrupted, "He genuinely is a reporter—an independent one, not affiliated with any publication."

The man dismissed my defense with a snort. "We don't acknowledge such journalists." I shrugged, indicating resignation. "What about your identities?" he pressed, eyes narrowing.

Feigning casualness, I gestured to Flora. "She's a middle school teacher, and I work at a university library."

He skimmed through a folder, heightening my apprehension, then snapped it shut. "We don't accept that Harlan Brown is mentally ill. We suspect deliberate sabotage, hence his detention for investigation. You should cease your search to avoid further complications."

His words left me exasperated. "A friend disappears, and we can't look for him?"

"You now know his whereabouts. Once he clarifies everything, there will be a resolution."

Flora sighed. "Given his mental state, can you at least share what he's said?"

The man deliberated, then whispered with his colleagues. One exited the room, leaving us in a tense silence, the air thick with unspoken threats. I was relieved Harlan Brown hadn't resorted to using the lethal device from the assassins.

As the silence stretched on, I asked, "What are we waiting for?"

The man's reply was curt and detached. "We're seeking approval from our superiors regarding your request."

I acknowledged the man's warning with a simple "Oh," and we settled back into that oppressive silence, the weight of which felt heavier with each passing minute. The man eventually broke the silence, engaging us in conversation. We tread carefully, mindful not to say anything that could be misconstrued as "nonsense," the very accusation that had ensnared Harlan Brown.

After an interminable half-hour, the man who had left earlier returned, whispering something to his superior. Even mundane exchanges here were shrouded in an air of secrecy.

The man nodded and gestured for us to follow him into another room.

This new room was stark, save for a few chairs and a television. Our guide gestured for us to sit. "You'll see footage of Harlan Brown's actions here. Remember, this is confidential. If you disclose it, you'll be considered an enemy."

I nodded, acknowledging the gravity of his warning. The man tapped the wall, and the TV flickered to life, displaying the entrance of a grand building. A group emerged, led by a tall, formidable middle-aged man in dark glasses. As another group of reporters approached, Flora nudged me—there was Harlan Brown, blending in with the journalists.

Tension coiled in my stomach. The man in sunglasses was a significant figure, and though not Harlan Brown's primary target, an impulsive move against him could spell disaster.

The scene was cacophonous, with reporters clamoring for attention. The main figure's voice cut through the din, confident and unbothered. "What are you afraid of?" he challenged.

The screen froze. Our guide pointed, "What follows was cut from the news."

Flora and I murmured in unison, acknowledging the gravity of what we were about to see. The footage resumed, and we watched as Harlan Brown stepped forward, his voice rising above the crowd. "Of course I'm afraid. I'm afraid you'll destroy an entire city!"

The main figure turned away, disdain evident even behind his sunglasses. In a flash, two nondescript men flanked Harlan Brown, expertly restraining him. They applied pressure to his waist, sapping his strength and dragging him away.

Despite this, Harlan Brown's voice rang out, defiant. "Don't think it's your decision. You're not in control. You're being manipulated by something beyond you—by those stones, you—" His words were abruptly cut off as he disappeared from view. The main figure continued unfazed, addressing the remaining reporters before retreating inside. The screen went dark.

The room was silent once more, the reality of Harlan Brown's plight hanging heavily in the air. Flora and I exchanged a glance, understanding the peril he was in and the daunting task that lay ahead of us.

The moment the TV screen went dark, I couldn't contain my frustration. "This is absurd! If he's simply responding to questions, how is that nonsense?"

The man's expression hardened, "It absolutely is."

I was about to argue further when Flora subtly signaled me to hold back. "Harlan Brown mentioned being influenced by a big stone. What could that possibly mean? It's baffling."

Her words made me pause. While Harlan Brown's claim might sound nonsensical to others, Flora and I knew his cryptic reference to the influence of celestial bodies. But her question was a strategic move, and I quickly caught on. "Yes, it's just the ramblings of his intermittent mental illness," I agreed, feigning exasperation. "Poor Harlan Brown."

The man scrutinized me with suspicion, and I played my part, shaking my head as if lamenting Harlan Brown's condition.

After a moment, the man said, "No one understands his ramblings. Post-arrest, he insisted he could reveal a shocking secret about astrology if he saw the top leader."

I couldn't help but smile wryly. Harlan Brown certainly had a vivid imagination. "Naturally, you materialists wouldn't entertain such nonsense."

The man replied, "His actions have already caused a degree of disruption."

"Questioning and answering shouldn't equate to harm. If you don't want answers, why ask?" I countered.

He snapped, "You can't just answer however you please."

"I understand," I said, feigning compliance. "Responses must align with expectations. Harlan Brown was too naive."

The man studied me intently, and I met his gaze, unwavering. "I'm simply speaking my mind."

His demeanor remained stern. "We've conducted a thorough investigation and, of course, won't grant him an audience with the leader."

Flora and I exchanged a glance of relief. She inquired, "Did the investigation yield any conclusions?"

He paused, then replied, "He's been declared persona non grata and will be expelled shortly. There's no need for you to remain here."

A wave of relief washed over me. "Understood. We'll wait for him at the border."

The man continued to scrutinize us, his gaze penetrating. It was unsettling, but eventually, he relented. "Someone will escort you out."

That night, Flora and I left the city.

Two days later, as we waited at the border, I spotted Harlan Brown being escorted by two armed guards. Relief and anticipation mingled as we prepared to reunite with our friend and navigate whatever lay ahead.

CHAPTER 13

FATE

arlan Brown's demeanor was a mix of defeat and defiance as he approached us, eyes brimming with tears. "I failed," he confessed, but quickly added, "But at least I've made the world aware of the impending destruction of a city."

His determination was admirable, and I hesitated to shatter his belief, but he needed to understand the reality. Gently, I said, "You haven't achieved that. Remember, television footage can be manipulated."

His face fell, a silent "Ah" escaping his lips as he absorbed the blow. Flora stepped in, her voice soothing, "Let's talk more when we're safe. Your courage demonstrates the strength of your character, and you're undeniably our best friend."

Her words kindled a spark of hope in his eyes, and he wiped his tears. "I failed, Ash. Will you... take risks again?"

I shook my head decisively. "No, because actions like yours won't change anything."

As I spoke, my gaze drifted to the "ring" on his finger—a sophisticated weapon from the assassin's arsenal. Harlan Brown, fueled by frustration, yanked it off and hurled it into the road. I moved to stop him, but it was too late. The ring was crushed under a truck tire, vanishing without a trace.

I sighed, "Tens of thousands of dollars gone. What a waste."

Harlan Brown replied bitterly, "Money means nothing. It's my lack of courage I regret."

I quickly countered, "I disagree."

He lamented, "I answered 'what are you afraid of' with conviction. I should have acted, even if it meant targeting a secondary goal."

Flora shook her head, "That's naive and reckless. It wouldn't have achieved anything."

I echoed her sentiment, "Exactly."

Despondent, Harlan Brown asked, "So what should we do?"

Neither Flora nor I had an answer. Over the following days, we discussed this dilemma with Harlan Brown, but clarity eluded us.

Harlan Brown remained steadfast in his belief that Theo Thomas's assertion—that the disaster could be averted—was true. He even proposed various strategies to address the issue at its root, driven by his belief in the possibility of change.

Harlan Brown's struggle against the seemingly unchangeable influence of the stars is both fascinating and poignant. It's a testament to human curiosity and the desire to exert control over forces that seem beyond our grasp. His ideas, while imaginative, highlight the tension between human ambition and the limitations of our current technology and understanding.

The notion of stars influencing human behavior is an age-old concept found in astrology and various cultural beliefs. While modern science doesn't support this idea, it serves as a rich metaphor for the unseen forces that shape our lives.

Harlan Brown stood before me, his eyes alight with a fervor that bordered on obsession. "Imagine," he began, "if we could alter the very fabric of the cosmos. The seven stars of the Black Dragon Constellation hold sway over human destiny. Shift them slightly, and you shift the minds they control."

I nodded, intrigued yet skeptical. "I see your point, Harlan. But tell me, how do you propose we nudge these celestial giants?"

His enthusiasm remained undeterred. "Theoretically," he declared, "a missile aimed at the stars. A collision and subsequent explosion upon the surface of a celestial body would suffice to create that shift."

I sighed, the weight of reality pressing down. "Harlan, we lack the technology. No rocket exists that can traverse the vastness to reach the Black Dragon's stars. Not now, and likely not for generations."

Harlan's eyes flickered, determination undimmed. "Then perhaps an asteroid—a cosmic slingshot to knock the stars from their course."

Yet even as he spoke, doubt crept in. He shook his head, the impracticality dawning. "What force could redirect an asteroid's path?"

A silence fell, broken only by Harlan's sudden inspiration. "Perhaps we send emissaries—silver-tongued envoys—to persuade those under celestial forces to relent, allowing our cities to thrive."

But hope faded as quickly as it appeared. "No," he lamented, "their power is absolute. Mere words cannot unbind the chains of destiny forged by the stars. We are but instruments of a greater mystery."

After exhausting every avenue, I interjected, "Consider this: Theo Thomas, a master observer of the heavens, dedicated his life to understanding the stars' influence. Yet, he never altered a single path of fate."

Harlan's eyes widened. "Are you saying..."

I continued, "The celestial signs are warnings, whispers of inevitability. Even if the chosen few discern them and shout them from the rooftops, the outcome remains unchanged. The stars' decree is immutable."

Harlan's face fell. "Then why did Theo Thomas burden you with this quest?"

I sighed, a heavy truth settling between us. "Age clouds his judgment. He believes salvation is within reach, but it is beyond us."

Yet Harlan's spirit was unbowed. "Surely, there must be a way. Not everything is set in stone."

I offered a wry smile. "So, Harlan, what ingenious scheme will you conjure next?"

Harlan Brown waved his hand animatedly, "Consider Pompeii, obliterated nearly 1,900 years ago. If someone had forewarned its people, urging them to flee, imagine the lives spared. The city would still succumb to volcanic wrath, but its people could escape the clutches of death."

His excitement was palpable. "We could apply this strategy here—warn the residents of this doomed city to evacuate before it's too late."

Flora and I exchanged a somber glance and sighed in unison.

Harlan Brown frowned, puzzled. "Why the hesitation? Isn't this a viable plan?"

I nodded slowly. "Yes, but there's no need for proclamations. This isn't an abrupt catastrophe like Pompeii's. The decline of this city will be slow, visible to all. Those who can leave, will. Ironically, the more who flee, the swifter the city's demise. Isn't that the truth?"

Harlan Brown stood silent, absorbing the gravity of my words. Finally, he mused aloud, "What do you call something that is destined to happen, yet remains unchangeable?"

Flora and I responded in unison, "Fate."

The night had deepened into midnight. Harlan Brown wandered into the courtyard, eyes drawn skyward to the brilliant constellations. He gestured at the heavens with a bitter smile, "The eastern stars, they truly form a dragon. This dragon... this dragon..."

Flora and I stood behind him, pondering. "The connection between these celestial bodies and human thoughts and actions? It's too enigmatic. We recognize the patterns but cannot grasp their essence."

Harlan Brown murmured, "Someday, the truth will be revealed."

I asked softly, "How distant is that 'someday'?"

Silence enveloped us all—Harlan Brown, Flora, and me—each lost in the vastness of the night and the mysteries it held.

▼ Extra Message

"Chasing the Dragon" is a narrative that defies the conventional expectation of a neatly wrapped conclusion. It's a reminder that not all stories need an endpoint, a resolution, or even a clear message. Life, after all, is filled with loose ends and unanswered questions, and this story embraces that uncertainty.

In past tales, Ash Morris has always been a man of action, achieving success or facing failure. But in "Chasing the Dragon," Ash finds himself in a unique position—doing nothing. It's a stark portrayal of the reality that not everything in life is within our grasp, no matter the effort we expend. Some pursuits, like the dragon itself, remain elusive and unattainable.

So, what does "Chasing the Dragon" seek to convey? Perhaps, it's that not every story must impart a lesson or reveal a profound truth. There are countless narratives that simply exist, reflecting the complexity and ambiguity of the human experience.

And who is "Chasing the Dragon" written for? It's not tailored for those seeking straightforward answers or clear-cut morals. Instead, it speaks to those who are comfortable with ambiguity, who appreciate the journey rather than the destination.

Yet, despite its complexities, "Chasing the Dragon" remains accessible. It's a story that resonates on an intuitive level, inviting readers to reflect on their own quests and the dragons they chase.

You've grasped its essence, haven't you? Undoubtedly.